TALES OF THE LOST SCHOONER

A middle grade historical novel

By Sandy Carlson

The Merry Viking Publishing House LLC

ISBN-10: 1492184640
ISBN-13: 978-1492184645

The Merry Viking Publishing House LLC
P.O. Box 1020, Battle Creek, MI 49016
www.themerryvikingpublishinghouse.com

DEDICATION

To my story-telling hero, Jeffrey

ACKNOWLEDGMENTS

With thanks to the Blue Quills Writers Group
and the Write Ladies for Critters.

Thanks to Lake Superior Port Cities Inc. and Frederick Stonehouse
for his research for the stories rewritten here on pages
48, 50, 58ff, 74ff, and 86.

Thanks to the many Great Lakes marine museums and their workers
who awe and inspire me with their displays and teachings.

And always, thanks to my husband and boys and family and friends
for their never-ending support.

CONTENTS
for
TALES OF THE LOST SCHOONER

Chapter One
ON THE STREET

"I'm going with the Reverend Brace's group," Sissy said. "And I'm taking Bridget with me. There ain't nothing you can do about it, Honor Patrick Sullivan. Nothing to say to change my mind."

Sissy's eyes focused on me. We sat on the alley stoop we now called home. With her arms folded tight, she looked more like our mother than a ten-year-old street urchin. Our eight-year-old sister didn't say a word. She kept her big scared eyes on Sissy. I wasn't sure if I was happy with the fact that Reverend Brace and his Children's Aid Society fed us, or if I hated him for filling Sissy and Bridget's heads full of hopeful nonsense. We were family. You could easily tell we Sullivans were related with our red hair and freckled faces. I could take care of them. Hadn't I been doing just that?

"No family's going to take in three orphans," I pointed out. "Or even two."

"We ain't orphans, Honor," Bridget wailed as she twisted Sissy's pinafore. "Mummy's alive."

I bit my lower lip and looked away so Bridget wouldn't see inside me like she always did. Sure, our mother was alive.. After Father disappeared, she struggled to keep our younger four siblings and us fed by selling rags on the streets of New

York City. I didn't like to think about the nights. She couldn't feed us all. She kicked the three of us older children out of the apartment, saying we had better luck surviving on the streets than in our own home. Now our home was a cold stone stoop. We weren't the only stoop-dwellers.

I hated Mama. She was as good as dead to me, just like Father, although no one knows what happened to him. My job was to take care of Sissy and Bridget. After all, twelve-years-old is practically a man, and I had me a fine job of selling newspapers as long as Chas didn't crowd over towards my corner to snag some of my customers. I made a steady enough income. There was always news. Always people who hungered for the latest. And their hunger is what fed us Sullivans.

The cool, salty wind blew in off the Atlantic Ocean. I couldn't quench the nagging feeling that the late September winds were bringing change with them. If I could figure out how to stow us away on a ship heading back to Ireland, I would. I bet one of our relations would take us in. The famine there is long gone.

I pushed my brown wool cap off my forehead, a new-to-me cap which one of my rich customers gave me since it didn't fit him. It didn't quite fit me, either. It hung over both my ears, it made customers notice me as more than a street kid, and at night it kept Bridget's head warm.

I peeled my potato and cut it into three pieces for our supper.

"We're doing okay between the Five Points Mission for lunch, and my job," I said. "Besides, I get paid tomorrow. You get some school-learning there at the Mission." I hated bringing up the very place which put silly thoughts into my sisters' heads about new families.

Sissy wasn't as convinced of our good fortune, nor about

me providing for them.

"Police rounded up more children today, Honor," she said. "Took them to prison and stuck them in with adults. What if that happened to us while you're out selling? Would you visit us in jail?"

Bridget squirmed. I could tell she was torn. I wrapped my arm around Bridget and kissed the top of her fuzzy red head. She smiled up at me. I'd protect her. I'd protected them both so far. As Bridget nibbled on her potato and she calmed down, Sissy started up again.

"Reverend Brace said the children who agreed to go out west would be placed in good church-going families out in Michigan, families waiting for children to help them. We could be in a family, Honor. Eat at a table."

"Have a new Mummy and Daddy?" Bridget plugged in. Her eyes glistened with hope.

I'd heard the guff from Reverend Brace before. It was a ploy to get rid of us street kids by placing us out to work for farmers. He used the words "new employers" as often as he used the word "new parents." No one in New York or in Michigan was going to adopt three of us. We'd survived on the city streets for four months now. We would survive the winter. These streets held familiar bricks, familiar sounds, familiar smells. The other newsies weren't any better or worse off than we were. The streets and alleys and abandoned buildings were full of us children. But we were survivors. We'd be just fine.

"No," I said at last.

Sissy folded her arms again and her potato piece rolled off her dress and onto the alley.

Bridget leaned her head against me and said, "Sing us a song, Honor."

***

One month later, on the morning of September 28, 1854, ladies from the newly formed Children's Aid Society gave the three of us Sullivans and forty-four others under the age of fifteen, new clothes and shoes and a cardboard suitcase for our journey to Michigan.

New!

Maybe giving in to Sissy wasn't going to be so bad after all. And maybe Reverend Brace was telling the truth.

Maybe.

Chapter Two
ERIE CANAL

Mr. Smith, our escort for the trip, led us to the wharf where we boarded a Hudson River side-wheeler steamship called *Isaac Newton*. The captain gave each of us a berth to sleep in and blankets, real blankets, for the overnight trip to Albany. I can't remember the last time I felt a blanket over me at night. Unsold newspapers are just as warm, but they're also noisy.

"If I could, I'd adopt the forty-seven of you children," the captain told us.

I liked him and wished he could adopt us all, at least three of us. Wouldn't that make for a grand old life, floating up and down the Hudson River every day, and in our own berths under a blanket every night?

Sissy wanted to be part of a real family again, on land. She looked out over the river, and then smiled at me. Getting out of New York City suited her well.

"This is the farthest west I've ever been," she said.

I hadn't quite forgiven her for forcing us on this trip. Yet, I had to admit there was something heart-thumping about not knowing what lay ahead, and to be hopeful about it. For now, we had food and beds, real beds, or rather, boat berth beds, which were just as good. Nights on our city stone stoop had chilled our poor Bridget causing her to shiver and whimper in her sleep.

The boat captain shook each of our hands as we left him We marched down the canal and piled aboard the barge heading up the newly built Erie Canal on to Buffalo. Mules pulled barges up and down the canal, led by their drivers walking next to them. I walked along the path next to the canal with some of the older boys, including Chas, the only other Newsie who'd volunteered for this adventure.

"This is better than selling newspapers," Chas said watching the puffy clouds overhead, and tripping on the gravel at his feet. Maybe he wasn't used to his new shoes.

One of the mule drivers said that singing kept his Ole Sally happy.

"I like to sing," I told him.

The driver sang to Chas and me about the Erie Canal and a mule called Sal. After hearing the chorus once, we joined him each time it came around.

"Someone wrote that song about my Sal," he said. "There ain't any other mules by that name anywheres from Albany to Buffalo."He sang the last part of his sentence.

I never knew anyone before who had a song written about them, not even a mule.

One of our uncles, Bartholomew Sullivan, helped build the canal. He'd stayed on in Buffalo when it finished. Mama considered him a wild drunkard. I wonder what she would think of her wild children passing so near our wild uncle. I wondered if Uncle Bartholomew looked like Father. I bet I'd know him if I saw him. People always said I looked like Father. And who could tell? Maybe Uncle Bartholomew had settled down from his wild ways and married a pretty little Irish lass, and would like the use of three really helpful and clean street urchin relatives all the way from New York City.

We piled off the barge and walked along to the harbor like forty-seven ducks in a row, each with our small cardboard suitcases in hand. But we were tough New York kids. It was easy to tell this part of Buffalo wasn't much different from where we'd come from.

"Stay together, children," Mr. Smith piped as he stood tall and hurried us past buildings with women hanging out of the second floor windows, women calling to us boys to come on up and join them. One ancient man on the street woke. He blinked his eyes from his drunken sleep and started singing, "Buffalo gals, won't you come out tonight," before falling back against his brick wall with a thwack. Mr. Smith hurried us on past.

We never had the chance to discover if Uncle Bartholomew was still in Buffalo.

Several side-wheel steamers were tied along the docks. Schooners, sloops, and barks filled the harbor with their masts sticking skyward like a forest with no leaves on the trees. Mr. Smith stopped once to ask directions and we headed toward one of them, a schooner named the *City of Cheektowaga*.

Sissy planted her feet firmly on the dock before boarding. "Now," she said, "this is the farthest west I've ever been."

Bridget clung to her arm, and we boarded the boat.

Chapter Three
THE *CITY OF CHEEKTOWAGA*

Ships around us squeaked as their wood pulled against their ropes tied to the dock. Other ropes with metal hooks clinged and clanged softly against the masts. A quiet lap-lap-lap sounded as small waves touched the sides of the boat. Beyond the harbor lay the sea – Lake Erie, they called it, full of waves topped in white. I guessed the land on the north was Canada.

I stretched my neck up at our center mast. It wasn't as tall as New York City buildings, but it made me feel dizzy. The American flag, with all thirty-one stars on it, flapped proudly from it. There were two other masts in front and three decks. A long red triangular flag flew on the forward mast. Since we were three Sullivans, I took this as a good sign. Maybe I had made the right choice after all by agreeing we should come on this trip.

Mr. Smith planned to head upbound from here to Detroit, Michigan. Then we'd board a train for our final destination, a town with the odd name of Dowagiac.

"I've never been on a train before," Sissy said.

"Me, neither," piped in Bridget.

A young man straddled the boom which ran horizontal to the big mast. He whistled as he sewed part of the white flax sail in front of him with a large curved needle. I wondered how a sail got torn in the first place.

A small iron stove sat in front of the center mast. A man shaped like a barrel adjusted a skillet and tied it down with rope. He took one look at us and looked away, spitting a wad of black tobacco over the side of the boat. I wasn't sure it was going to clear the railing to land in water.

"This sure is a big boat," Bridget said.

"Ship!" spat a young man standing by the ropes going up a mast. His eyes were wide and he chewed on his fingernails. "She's a ship and you are bad luck to speak more ill of her." He looked at two stern-looking men with bushy beards at the back of the ship near the wheel. "She's going to sink soon," he whispered to no one in particular.

Bridget looked at me with her eyes welling up. Brave girl that she was, not a single tear fell. I squeezed her hand.

"It'll be okay," I said to her. "They wouldn't let us on board if it wasn't safe."

Cattle mooed below us, and the stink of animals floated upward through the large open hatch near them.

"See? Even the cows are mooing how excited they are to get out on the lake." Sissy rolled her eyes at me. I agreed, my comment sounded silly. Bridget smiled, so I guessed it wasn't so silly after all.

An old man of about thirty pointed to the front hatch and piped at us, "Climb down backwards, facing away from the ladder."

About half the size of the one at the back, only one person could go through this hatch at a time. Mr. Smith went down first, rather unsteadily, followed by some of the boys. Bridget squished into me.

"I don't want to," she whispered. "I'm scared."

"Get on down there into the steerage," said Barrel Man.

He grinned at Bridget, "Or we'll strap you to the sails for the duration." He swung a threatening coil of rope in his hand.

"I can go down the right way," Chas said. "Watch." He procceded to leap into the hatch opening face forward. He slipped on the second rung, wacked his head on the hatch edge, and tumbled to the deck below. Pigs squealed. Bridget buried her face in my jacket.

I eyed the sailor shaking the rope at us. I took a deep breath, held Bridget firmly in front of me. "I'll go down first. That way I'll catch you if you fall. Watch your head."

I let go of her and winked at Sissy. I faced backwards like we were instructed, and climbed down with no problems. It was dark. The poignant aroma of cow and pigs filled my nostrils. Bridget came next, and then Sissy. Even in their full dresses, both made it down the ladder with no problem.

Along with the twenty or so cattle on this level were some pigs, all fenced in. The pigs and cows looked about as happy being there as we children did. Beyond them was a wall with a door. Mr. Smith listened and nodded to one of the bushy-bearded men who opened the door. Inside was a passageway with doors to either side, probably cabins. The *City of Cheektowaga* was apparently a cargo and passenger ship. Mr. Smith returned to us and pointed to the opening leading to the deck yet below this one.

"Down the hatch you go," Mr. Smith said.

I guessed there were more cabins on the lowest level of the ship, the steerage, I heard the sailor call it. I was wrong. The steerage was one large hold, three-quarters of it filled with coal.

Mr. Smith got one of the staterooms above us, next to the cows and pigs. Our accommodations were in the steerage along with the coal. A single amber lantern hung on a post near the ladder. It took a while for my eyes to adjust to the darkness.

The walls of the ship – the hull – curved for us to sit or lay down right underneath the animals. We older boys distributed three bales of hay for us all to sit or sleep upon. At least, we assumed it was for us and not for the ton of coal, nor for the animals above us. Although perhaps it was meant for the animals.

Bridget and Sissy huddled next to me as we started out. We broke out our crackers and cheese lunch provided by the Children's Aid Society. I'd never admit it out loud, but I felt trapped in the bottom of the ship. I hated not being able to see where we were going or what the water looked like.

The ship lurched and tipped some to the side. Sissy screamed. Bridget clutched onto me.

"It's just the wind filling our sails," I told them. I hoped it was just the wind filling our sails. "And riding tilted like this is like being in a Fun House. See? We just have to get our balance."

"I don't like Fun Houses," Bridget said, even though she'd never been in one.

Lake Erie wasn't the same traveling water as the Hudson River or the Erie Canal. We started out tilted, but sooth sailing. Soon Lake Erie quickly became choppy as we crashed through wave after wave.

"I wish we were allowed up top where we could see light and the horizon," Chas said. "It helps keep everyone from puking.

He said that right before he vomited on Bridget, who in turn vomited on the straw. I gagged and drew the girls away from Chas, wishing he'd stayed back in New York City.

The farm animals directly over us. If the floorboards would have been fitted tighter, it would have made a huge difference. Those poor animals were as sick as we were. Their diarrhea flowed through the cracks and dribbled onto us.

We had a bucket of water to wash with on our night day sail. Half of it sloshed out before we could wash anything off.

"Look," I said quietly to Chas. I pointed to the water swishing around the ballast near us.

Chas' eyes popped opened. "It leaks!"

"Shh," I said squeezing his arm. "You'll frighten the girls."

"I'll frighten me," he answered. "I'll let Mr. Smith know."

He scrambled up the ladder while I pulled the girls closer to me. I kept my eye on that water lapping inside the ship. Chas returned in a couple minutes. He didn't speak for a long time. I kept urging him with my eyes to talk to me, but to share it in a way so as not to frighten my sisters, of course.

"Has it gotten any higher?" he said at last.

I shook my head.

"Mr. Smith said all ships leak. If the water gets too deep, they'll just pump it out. Standard procedure, he tried to assure me." We both rolled our eyes.

"Well, at least they'll know, from us, when the water starts covering their coal," I said.

Chas smirked. It was a good thing that Reverend Brace taught us how to pray.

Mr. Smith convinced the captain to allow us up on deck during a calm stretch. We went up five children at a time, although some boys were too sick to climb the ladders.

As I stood with the breeze to our stern, the wind scooped my cap off my head. I reached for it. My fingers brushed it. I ended up whacking it further over the side of the ship and down into the water. I put my hands on the railing to jump in after it.

"Don't try it," said a crew member about nineteen years old. He was the sail-mender in Buffalo. He sat on the deck working at a piece of rope. "Lake Erie may be the shallowest of the Great Lakes, but it's still deep enough to swallow whole ships. Besides, not meaning to scare you or anything, but the captain probably wouldn't turn back for you."

I whipped my hands off the railing. What was I thinking? I didn't even know how to swim. I watched my new cap from my old life float along.

Chapter Four
KNOTS AND KNOCKING

My cap drifted along with us for a while as if it was as reluctant to leave me as I was it. That was the only thing I really owned. The ladies of the Children's Aid Society gave each of us "orphans" new clothes for the journey and a cardboard suitcase. I wore my old shoes, but put the new ones they bought me in the suitcase. We pulled ahead of my cap and our schooner's wake dragged it beneath the sea. I watched the spot, thinking somehow it would resurface. It never came back up. I wondered how many other caps lined the bottom of Lake Erie.

My sisters and two other boys spent their topside time giving up their lunches to the fish. So far, I was the only one of us forty-seven who came topside who didn't use the time to hang over the railing and puke. For a few minutes, I rubbed my sisters' backs and sang some lines from "the Meeting of the Waters" and "Lilly Dale" and "Cape Cod Girls." I could only get a couple lines out before they waved me off. I'd thought they just didn't like those particular songs, but it seemed they didn't like any song at the moment, at least not watery songs.

I stood tall in the fresh air, taking in deep breaths upwind of my fellow retching passengers. I wanted to do anything except watch or listen to them. I walked up to the crewmember playing with ropes. His plaid shirt and wool black trousers were new, too. I wondered if someone like the Children's Aid Society gave him his clothes.

"So what's that over there?" I pointed to a tall round building behind us on the land.

"Marblehead Point," he answered. "The oldest light on these Great American Lakes."

"Is it made out of marble?" I asked.

The crewmember grinned and shook his head.

"You've got a sailor's voice," he said. "I heard you singing to those girls. You have a much better voice than me. The captain almost didn't hire me because of it."

I wasn't sure if he told the truth or was just making conversation. I shrugged and thanked him for the compliment. He wove on his section of rope.

"Is there anything I can do to help?" I asked.

"You know how to make knots?"

"I know how to tie my shoes." I laughed since I stood before him barefooted. He didn't laugh. "I'm Honor," I said, holding out my hand, a hand which was worse than dirty. He may have considered taking it, but nodded with a smile.

"William," he said. "Watch,"

He proceeded to twist the rope around and under and around again until he'd woven an interesting knot pattern. He tossed the bit of rope at me. I examined the twists and turns.

"It's called a Turk's Head. Takes some time to get it right. Try it." He pulled out another stretch of rope to make another knot.

I caught the knot and started to pull it apart. I tied it right back in order to understand how to do it. I kept playing with it, weaving and unweaving.

The nail-biting man wandered near us, muttering. "I've got to get off this black cat." He pulled at a sail line and re-knotted it, gurgling his words. He looked about the ship. His looks darted all over the place. His eyes finally stopped on me. They were filled with fear and desperation. "She's gonna sink," he whispered. I wasn't even certain that he saw me. "Six is unlucky. And Friday. Why did Klaus make us leave on a Friday? Must get off." I followed his look to a small boat tied down near the front of our vessel.

William noticed me looking at the muttering man. "Pay him no mind," William said. "Harold is a superstitious Nervous Nellie."

The man Harold jerked back to look at William.

"She's gonna sink," he insisted. "Mark my words. I feel it in my bones. The lake will take her. It will." He gnawed on his thumb nail as Barrel Man put an arm around him and pulled him away. Barrel Man cast me a suspicious look.

"Don't you listen to them land-loving street rats," Barrel Man said to the other. "I'll keep you safe, Harold."

William kept his eyes lowered, onto his knots. I did the same with mine. When the two others were out of sound's reach, I asked

"Is he going to abandon ship?" I asked.

William looked up from his knot making and after Harold. "Probably not. At least not now. It's safer aboard a larger ship than that yawl, and Harold knows it. One big wave could wash over her, and – plop – when she goes turtle, there fulfills his silly superstition. Jack's been worrying him with his tales of surviving two shipwrecks." William shook his head. "Surviving should be the key word, not wreck," he said.

After listening to nervous Harold I found I had knots in my stomach. I closed my eyes and let the breeze wash over me. The wind blew away fear of past, present and future. I opened my eyes. Harold and Barrel Man were gone. Only my sisters still hanging over the ship's railing.

"Friday?" I asked William.

"Sailor superstition," he answered with his head wobbling.

"Aren't you a sailor?"

"Just for this voyage, Milwaukee to Buffalo and back home to Milwaukee. I wanted to see what it was like out here. Experience the world and all before settling down, you know."

I wondered if there were any older, more experienced sailors aboard who weren't terrified. The bearded captain and first mate were either stern or terrifying. I assumed they were competent sailors.

"So what's superstitious about Friday?" I asked him.

"It's bad luck to start a season or even a sea journey on a Friday. We left Buffalo on a Friday, you know. Plus," William continued, "this ship's been renamed. Apparently, it wasn't done properly."

"There's a proper way to rename a ship?"

William shrugged. He wore a disbelieving smile.

"So what are there six of?" I asked. Three masts and three decks make six, but that didn't make sense. You could add lots of things together aboard to make six.

"Us." William waved his hand over the ship. "Captain Klaus, his first mate, Finbarr, and us four deckhands. The unlucky six. Ooooo."

I chuckled along with William's disbelief.

"Get the next group up," spoke a bearded man behind us. It was first mate Finbarr.

"Yes, sir," William said, leaping to his feet.

I held out the knotted rope to William. He waved the back of his hand at me and walked towards the hatch. The bearded man's eyes pierced through me and then he looked me over from head to toe as though he were considering something. I looked down at my clothes soiled with vomit and excrement, and nearly lost it like the other children. Instead, I turned my face to the wind and sucked in one last deep breath before I put the rope knot around my wrist to take it down the two ladders to the lower deck. I would learn how to make that Turk's Head knot.

Returning to our stinking hold made the short trip topside almost unbearable. Down in the steerage section, Sissy and Bridget hugged each other and cried. I knew their stomachs must ache from all their vomiting. I hadn't done a very good job of taking care of them.

It struck me that we hadn't even let our mama know we'd left New York. I wondered if she would even care. Reverend Brace and his people told us to make a break with our past and not think about the people or places we knew. I wasn't sure I wanted to remember a mama who abandoned us. I kissed both my sisters on the tops of their heads, and they hugged me just as we got dripped with cow urine.

I played with my bit of rope, tying it and untying it until I could form the knot without having to even see to work it in light.

As the boat rocked and creaked, and the animals moaned and groaned, none of us got much sleep. Sissy kept praying that we wouldn't die.

Chas looked pale. He caught me looking at him.

"Did you hear that?" he said.

"The cows stamping?"

"No. Chains. And that pitiful moaning. Don't you hear them? Listen." Chas tilted his head. "Rattling chains. And, there," he whispered. "Can't you hear it? Moaning. Ghosts," he said, and bobbed his head. "They want us. And look! We're leaking more." He pointed to the water near us.

Bridget buried her face in Sissy's dress.

The boat lurched to the side. Water from the ballast area splashed up onto us. Bridget wasn't the only one who screamed. Ghosts didn't scare me, but having the lake swallow us? Now that was something to worry about.

There were no chains on the boat. I'd only seen thick ropes. The only moaning going on would be Chas when I punched him in his stomach for scaring the girls.

Still, it was a distraction from our situation both in the bottom of the boat and the uncertainty of what our futures held. The boat straightened itself back up, just like it was supposed to do. I smiled at my sisters hoping my smile didn't look too fake.

"Whee," I said to Bridget.

She peeked at me from the corners of her eyes. I smiled bigger. Her lips twitched as if she considered smiling, too, and then buried herself back in Sissy's pinafore.

With the rocking and peeing and throwing up, all which seemed would never end, I realized we no longer rocked. Bridget noticed, too.

"Are we dead?" she asked. Her voice sounded thin in the pitch black of the hold.

"No, you stupid cow. We're near land," Chas said.

I swung at Chas and gave him that stomach punch I owed him. At least, I think it was Chas. He quit talking after my hit.

A lantern shone down the ladder followed by heavy sea boots and Barrel Man.

"Up you get, you street rats. Time to abandon ship."

Bridget started crying again. It didn't feel like we were sinking. The walls didn't leak as much now in the calmer sea. I put my arms calmly around my sisters and gave their shoulders each a confident squeeze.

"I bet we're in Michigan," I said to them.

Bridget looked up at me. Her big brown eyes sparkled in the lantern's amber light.

"Then," Sissy said straightening up, "this is the farthest west I've ever been. So far."

We climbed the two decks and stood on the deck under a cloudy sky. A misty rain fell about us in the late afternoon. A little bit of rain didn't bother us children none. We'd spent many days and nights on the streets of New York letting the rain wash us clean. Men herded the animals down a plank to the dock first – the pigs grunted into a wagon and a man linked the cows together with rope. Dock hands used pulleys and levers to lower empty wooden crates into the hold. I assumed it was for the coal. From this top deck height, we could look over the town of Detroit with its wooden buildings scattered on the other side of the warehouses.

"I wonder where we'll spend the night?" Sissy said.

Or eat, I thought.

"Are our new parents going to pick us up here?" Bridget added. "I hope they don't separate us. Please don't let them separate us, Honor."

"I don't know, Sissy. Don't worry, Bridget," I assured both my sisters. "I'll keep us together. From here, we head by train across Michigan to the frontier town of Dowagiac. Isn't that a fun word to roll around in your mouth? Dowagiac." I said that for Bridget's benefit. "And even if we are put with different families, it's got to be small enough a town that we'll see each other often enough."

"It's a farming community," Chas butt in. "We'll probably never see each other after they auction us off. Maybe some of these cows and pigs will be with us, though."

"What's auction mean?" Bridget asked.

"Sell us to the highest bidder," Chas answered.

Bridget's eyes went wide. "Our new parents are going to *buy* us?"

I wanted to punch Chas again. I refrained. He wasn't worth it. I knelt down to look Bridget in the face and wiped some of her matted hair to the side. I wiped my wet hand on my britches. "I promise you, both of you." I looked at Sissy, too. "We'll stay in the same family if we can. If not, we'll see each other often enough. I promised I'd look after you, didn't I?"

They both nodded.

From the beginning, I hadn't liked the idea of this placing out. We were safe enough on our doorstep in New York. Safe, as long as the police didn't do a roundup of street kids. Now as we neared our new destination, it was difficult to keep the butterflies in my stomach from fluttering up into my throat.

"And we'll see each other every Sunday," Sissy said. "All of the families who are picking us go to church and have letters from the pastor and a judge saying they are good people."

"Good people," Bridget repeated and leaned in to me for a hug.

"Time to get you urchins off," bellowed the first mate.

"Come along, children," Mr. White said, motioning for us to go down the plank to the dock. "Please wait down there for me. And, you – Honor, is it? Captain Klaus and I would like a word with you."

Chapter Five
SHANGHAIED

Bridget clung to my arm. I nodded to Sissy. She pulled Bridget, dragging her down the plank walk to the dock. They stood among the other children on the dock.

"Seems you've impressed the captain, Master Honor," Mr. White started.

I set down my suitcase and glanced at the captain, the bearded man who'd checked me over when I was topside learning the ropes with William. I looked to my battered shoes. The laces had many knots from breaking and unstringing to tie together. "Captain Klaus tells me that his sister in Alpena is looking for a fine young man who would help her with odd jobs around the house."

I jerked my head up to face a nodding Mr. White. We weren't in Dowagiac, and the suddenness of this change in plan clawed at my chest.

Over the rail my own sisters' eyes were larger than I'd seen before. I wanted to take them under my arms, hold tightly, and assure them it would be all right. We were getting placed with good families. That was our plan, right?

"… so you will remain aboard the *City of Cheek-ta*—"

"*Cheektowaga*," the captain inserted with a big grin. I felt numb. I couldn't read the expression of the captain since his full beard extended a good two inches out from his face. The first mate, Finbarr, in similar in dress and facial hair stood next to him. Finbar didn't smile, but slowly looked me over as if calculating something.

"God bless," Mr. White said abruptly. He shook my hand and joined the forty-six children waiting on the dock. My heart tumbled down the plank after him. Mr. White bent and whispered to my sisters. Their fearful eyes ground into my brain. I willed to change and fix the looks of abandonment on my sisters. Why couldn't I stay with them a little while longer, just until they were placed out? Then I could take the train to the Captain's sister's house. Just how far separated could we be?

Mr. Smith turned his back on me and herded the group away. Bridget screamed my name as she squirmed in Mr. White's hold. Sissy tagged along, holding onto Bridget's other hand.

"I will find you!" I shouted to my sisters. My last two words sounded more like a sob. Mr. Smith didn't look back. I bit my lips together.

A hand slapped hard on my back between the shoulder blades. The force nearly shoved me over the side. The Captain nodded and waved to the departing group. His hand gripped like a vice on my shoulder. After my sisters disappeared in the crowd, he finally released me.

"Well, son. You asked if there was anything you could do to help while aboard the *City of Cheektowaga*. Are you a lad of your word? We seem to be short a crew member."

My thoughts whirled. It took me a while to remember the context. Of course. It was the time they allowed us up on deck in the middle of the lake. I'd asked the older boy, William, if I could help. My Turk's Head rope knot remained in my suitcase with my new shoes. I'd meant to give it back to him.

Now I'd be able to.

I bobbled my head, praying the captain hadn't felt my trembling. I wasn't scared for me! I was scared for my sisters. I figured I didn't have much to say about the matter. Back in New York, I didn't want Sissy and Bridget going off to some distant frontier. Now they were alone.

So, how far away could Alpena be from Dowagiac? They were both in Michigan. We'd probably be able to see each other on Sundays when we attended church with our new families.

"Good lad," the captain said, still grinning. "Well, then you can earn your keep for traveling to my sister's by helping to swab down the decks. We have passengers coming aboard in a couple hours. We'll want her in ship-shape condition now, won't we?"

I nodded.

They call it shanghaied when the captain or first mate enlists a crew of drunks who sign their X for their name on a ship's roster, too drunk to know what they were getting into. I wasn't drunk. Captain Klaus and Mr. Smith were well aware I was a boy of twelve years who'd agreed to work for another family. I wasn't much more than a bit of product to be passed on. They must have figured if I'd agreed to work for some unknown family, I would be willing to be employed for the Captain's sister in a Michigan town called Alpena.

Four men washed down the top deck. I did not participate in that chore. Nor did I recognized them from the crew. The other workers must have been hired dock hands from Detroit.

Captain Klaus invited me to have some supper of ham and bread in his cabin. My stomach growled in response. Throughout the meal, the captain asked me lots of questions and seemed very interested in everything about me. He seemed so nice that I thought maybe he would tell me he wanted to adopt me for himself. Or if not, maybe his sister would like two hard-working girls as well. I could ask, later, when it was appropriate.

After our meal, he took me below deck.

Two more dock hands I didn't recognize scrubbed down the lower deck where the seasick cows and pigs had endured our sea adventure from Buffalo to Detroit next. I gagged, and then cleared my throat. I was glad I didn't have part of doing that chore. The fences were neatly piled, ready to be removed from the ship. We walked the length of the ship through a hallway with several passenger cabins to the left and right. Mr. Smith had slept in one of these. At the end of the hallway was a ladder going up and another one going down. The captain swung open the door beyond the ladders and said, "Crews' quarters." He shut the door before I could see.

My eyes twitched as we descended the ladder to the place with which I was most familiar. Both the coal and the other orphans were gone. I thought again of my sisters here in this hold along with the others from New York City streets. I didn't get much chance to think about them as muck from the upper two decks seeped down between the cracks and along the walls to this steerage level. The stench reeked so badly I thought my knees might give out from under me.

"You can wear these," the captain said, handing me a heavy pair of sea boots. I sat on a ladder rung, took off my battered shoes, and easily slipped the boots on over my bare feet. They were big. I laced them up really good to keep them on.

A crusty old sailor of about thirty years old with blackened teeth manned the water pump.

"Here ya go, Jack. Harold's gone. I brought you some

other help." Captain Klaus slapped me hard on my back once more and ascended the ladder, leaving Jack and me alone in the hold.

I mopped while Jack sat on a wooden crate, manning the bilge pump. He chewed a wad of tobacco and every once in a while spit the tobacco juice onto the floor, sometimes right where I'd just mopped. I'm sure the old guy was just careless with his aim.

Swishing and stirring around that dirt and other stuff made me sicker by the minute. I hadn't thrown up this whole sea trip. I did not want to do it now. Adding the strong smell of lye soap helped.

When we'd sufficiently cleaned the hold, I prepared to climb out of that place.

"Caulking," Jack said, tossing me a tin of pitch. Of course. The ship leaked. I mean, it wasn't just condensation on those planks. Lake water came in.

"How has this ship stayed afloat so long?"

"Don't you worry none about this ship," Jack said. "normal stuff this." He waved his hand at the wet hull. "I worked on a steamer before signing on with Klaus here. The steamer looked fine in dry dock, but each time we hit a wave, the planks separated just a bit. We didn't mind standing knee-deep in water in the engine room. As long as it didn't get high enough to get into the fire and put out the heat for steam, which it did."

"What happened?"

"Well," continued Jack. "We constantly pumped out the water till it was at an acceptable level, and then we hailed a passing steamer who towed us, until the line broke in a gale right near shore. The captain aimed us towards a sand bar where we nearly turtled. We all survived, except for the ship, that is."

I eyed him from the side, uncertain if he was telling the truth or not. If true, then he seemed awfully unlucky. I kept on caulking.

Finally done, we climbed to the middle deck, which remained damp from the cleanup.

A team of horses pulled a wagon next to our boat. We loaded our cargo of several barrels of some liquid and flour and corn bags. I helped the crew lower the cargo of bags and barrels of some liquid into the hold as our passengers boarded. They were made up mostly of rugged lumberjacks and a few quiet immigrant families and all their life possessions. The lumbermen settled into cabins while the Irish and German immigrants got the open area where the animals once were. No one had to go down into the hold even though it smelled nice and pretty now. The cabins were big enough for a walk to the ship's side and held two berths each two feet wide.

"Coil them ropes, boy," the first mate, Mr. Finbarr barked, pointing to the pile.

I wrapped the lines flat and in increasing circles on the deck.

A tug pulled us away from the dock. Another schooner threw us their bowline. After them came another sail, and another. The lead tug towed us four ships northward through the Detroit River. Tugs pulled other sailing vessels downbound. Steamers chugged past in the middle lane. The sounds of the flapping flags and cries sea gulls and of other sailors on nearby boats made it seem like I was back on a New York City street corner except this watery street was for ships. When we got onto Lake Sinclair where the lake opened up, we tossed lines back to the other boats and hoisted our sails. I learned by doing. I watched and did as the other crew did as Barrel Man sang a rhythm for us to respond to and heave to.

The rive widened into a large lake. Everyone here had a purpose. Everyone did something. Except for the passengers below., and the *City of Cheektowaga* rocked into each swell. I lost my balance a few times. After clinging to or sliding into the boom or railing, I picked up on how to sway along with the ship instead of against it.

"This be Lake St. Clair," Jack said. "William there says they named it that because that Frenchman LaSally discovered it on St. Clair's Day. He knows highfaluting stuff like that."

I never heard of LaSally, but did wonder what the lake was called before it had been discovered. Jack spit a wad of tobacco over the railing. It splashed into the saint's lake.

"You want to see where you'll be bunking down?"

I nodded.

The five-man crew stayed in a partitioned off section on that lower level, separated with a door, into one larger room with nine hammocks.

"There you go, lad." Jack pointed to the middle of three hammocks on top of each other with about two and a half feet between.

My own hammock! This would be so much better than a bunk. And there was a blanket that came with it, too. I'd heard about hammocks, I'd never been in one before. I knew we were under way and I probably ought to be on the top deck learning to tie sailor knots or something, I wanted to give my hammock a whirl. Instead it gave me a whirl and I landed on my face on the deck with the blanket over me.

Jack laughed as I rose, and then his eyes opened wide and he backed away. He scurried up the ladder and disappeared through the hatch to topside.

"You mess with my stuff, boy, and you better know how

to swim really good. Because if you mess with my stuff again, you'll find yourself alone some night in the water, trying to figure out which way to shore."

I looked up to see Barrel Man baring his crooked teeth at me.

Chapter Six
UPBOUND

The huge sailor bellowed, "Now get to where you belong, you scallywag."

I stood and backed up a step. How he slept in the small hammock, or even fit down the front hatch, was beyond my reckoning.

"But, the captain told me to stay on, until we reach his sister's in Alpena."

He straightened up, making him look even taller. "His sister?"

"Yes, sir. I mean, yes." He wasn't the captain. I guessed I should only call the captain "sir." I didn't see what came next. He swung his arm and slapped my face. Hard.

"I don't want no liar messing with my things."

I massaged my cheek, easing out the sting. "I… I'm sorry. I didn't know this was yours." I eyed the abandoned ladder. "And I'm no liar," I added, turning back to him. I didn't care if he was as large as the ship. I was no liar. "Ask the captain if you don't believe me."

"Captain? Our captain? The one with a sister? You're one of them crazy street kids. You get left behind?"

"Yes," I said straightening up tall myself, and then frowned. I'd meant yes only to the first part. "I mean, no."

He squinted at me. He started to raise his hand again. I flinched. He put his hand down and nodded. "Crazy. I'm guessing you're along, replacing young Harold. But know that you'll never be able to do that."

"Replacing? No. No. I'm on my way to be placed out with the captain's sister. Placed, not replacing." Now I could see how he'd erred.

"In Alpena?"

I nodded. Jeepers, this big guy sure was dense. I almost smiled, but eyed his massive hand and clearly thought better of it. I was a passenger on my way to Alpena. I got to sleep with the crew because I was practically part of the captain's family. All the passenger cabins were obviously spoken for. I wanted to reach out and say, "My name's Honor Sullivan. Pleased to make your acquaintance." I knew from being on the streets that making nice to strong people would help me later on. One squeeze from him and I was certain that every bone would break in my own hand. I scurried up the ladder as fast as I could to have a word with Jack.

When I got topside, I remembered my suitcase and went looking for where I'd left it by the dock plank. It was gone. The sailor William who showed me how to make a Turk's Head knot stood nearby.

"Have you seen my suitcase?" I asked. "It was right here."

William looked where I pointed. "I'm afraid the captain gave it to one of the immigrant men we dropped off in Detroit."

I widened my eyes at him.

"You mean—"

William shrugged apologetically.

My home, my cap, my sisters, all gone, and now even my

suitcase, although it was the latest of things I claimed as mine. I had nothing except the clothes on my back. A lump grew in my throat. Maybe if I jumped onto a tugboat and then ran after my sisters I could catch up with them. Maybe their train hadn't left for Dowagiac yet.

"Those boots will do well to keep you securely on deck. In fact, those are my old ones. But they gave me blisters. See? I got some new ones in Buffalo."

"Oh," I said, looking down at them. I wiggled my toes and wondered if I would also get blisters. With the laces pulled tight, they stayed on my feet just fine. William's boots looked the same as his old ones. A sailor must be paid a lot to be able to discard perfectly good boots to buy another pair.

Captain Klaus didn't make the lumberjacks stay below deck. I couldn't tell what made them so special. On the other hand, the immigrants, some who looked like they could be my red-headed relations, weren't allowed topside.

First mate Finbarr strode up to me.

"Steerage Boy, it's going to be your job to keep an eye on the bilge water."

I blinked, then answered, "How often do I check it?"

He looked disgusted by my question, as though even a simpleton street rat like me ought to know that answer.

"As often as it needs," he sneered.

The last time I'd been around the bilge pump was when in Detroit harbor when Tobacco Guy kept spitting on my clean hull before our passengers arrived.

I nodded. "Sure," I said and headed for the dark creaking prison. Even standing over the hatch and ladder to the lowest level brought back the pain of missing my sisters.

I lit a lantern hanging on a hook and started to descend. I wished Alpena would come quickly. It couldn't be too far

38

away now because some of the Germans were getting off there. Maybe I'd run away from the Captain's sister and find my way over to Dowagiac. How long would it take to hike there? First, I'd make sure Sissy and Bridget were safe, and then I'd see if anyone in the area needed an extra pair of hands around their farm. We'd be together again.

I sniffed. It smelled only faintly of excrement and vomit. We couldn't remove it completely from the ballast. Bags of flour and corn for lumber camps and settlements up north filled the center of the cargo hold. I wasn't sure I would want to eat any of that food.

I moved the bags away from the pump at the lowest part of the boat. All the while we traveled down here from Buffalo I didn't even know the pump was there, hidden by the ton of coal. When I checked between the ballast, I found about an inch or so of water. I frowned.

"I wonder if that's good," I said aloud.

"So far," came a soft low voice.

I turned to where I thought it came from. An old man about fifty years old peeked from behind a sack and then disappeared. I held the lantern high.

"I know you're there," I said. I stared where he'd disappeared.

A white haired man in tattered shirt and pants poked his head from behind a stack of flour bags. "Ye be seein' me, laddie?"

"Of course, I be seein' you, I mean, I can see you." He wasn't one of the crew. He had to be one of the passengers. "You scared me," I told him.

"Boooo," he said.

I started laughing so hard, I thought I'd drop the lantern. Burning the ship to the waterline wouldn't make too good an impression on the Captain, or his sister. It also would make getting over to Dowagiac a bit difficult.

"Ooooo," I answered with my eyebrows raised.

The old sailor looked me over from head to toe, just like Captain Klaus had. Only, I was pretty sure I wouldn't have to do whatever this man asked me to do.

"You better get back up the ladder to your people," I said.

"Ain't got no people," he answered slowly, turning his head and looking at me out of the sides of his eyes.

I knew some of what he was talking about.

"Maybe so," I said. "But you don't belong down here."

He sighed long and loud. I didn't know someone could hold that much air in their lungs.

"It be quieter down here, matie. Not busy-like or noisy as up top."

As much as I hated standing in the place where I spent hours with sick children from New York, including my sisters, I had to agree with him. It was more peaceful down here.

"Why do you talk like that?" I asked. "Like a pirate from one hundred years ago?"

"Argh," he answered.

I chuckled. "So, what's your name?" I asked.

"Name?" He looked up to the left and scratched at his scruffy beard like he was lost in thought. He finally grinned down to me. "You kin be callin' me Old Salty."

"Old Salty. Truth?"

"Aye. Truth, laddie." He studied me once more. An unexpected chill raced down my back. "En what ye be called?"

"Me? I'm Honor Patrick Sullivan from New York City."

"Shiver me timbers. That be an extra-long name from an fancy city."

I laughed. "Honor. Just call me Honor."

Old Salty nodded. "So, you ain't a'gonna be tellin' yer captain on me, now, are ye?"

Maybe he wasn't one of the passengers. Maybe he was a stowaway. I shook my head in answer to his question. "So where are you heading?"

"Wherever the wind takes me-like." He squinted at me and let out a long, low, "Argh."

I started laughing. This pirate-acting-stowaway lightened my spirit. It felt good to laugh again. I shook my head. "Just mind you don't go messing with the food shipment." Here I was, twelve years old, telling an old sailor what he could and couldn't do aboard a ship I'd only be on for a few more hours. I put my free hand on the ladder to start up.

"Er, laddie. Honor. Be tellin' me one thing."

"What's that?"

"Be ye believin' in ghosts?"

I laughed. "Oooo. Rattle. Rattle," I answered. "Oooo."

I climbed up to report to the first mate that there was an inch of water in the bulge, and that the pitch held out the lake water just fine. I'd not bother him with the fact that an old man was stowing away down in the hold. Old Salty, or whoever he was, seemed harmless enough. I also knew what it was like to be homeless. We had our city stoop. He could have the hold. Aye, he could be havin' it as long as he kept out of mischief. But if he be trouble, I'd have to make him walk the plank. Argh.

That night I slept in a swaying hammock directly below Barrel Man Bernard. By directly, I mean that his backside was only a couple inches from my chest. Once I got over the fact of not getting crushed – I prayed his hammock lines held – and of being in such close quarters, I let the sea rock me to sleep.

I dreamed about my sisters riding on a train. In the

dream, they walked forward through the train until they transformed into white wisps of smoke and funneled up the train's chimney stack. They disappeared somewhere over Michigan. Search as I might, Bridget and Sissy were gone.

Chapter Seven
LIAR, LIAR

The captain left William at the wheel. He stood tall with a grin on his face as wide as the sea. I sat topside with Jack learning the ropes.

"Knots are a sailor's trade," he informed me. "Try this one. It's a bread knot to hold the ends of two ropes together. Not to be confused with a granny knot." He showed me that one, too.

I worked on them until I could make the knots as smooth as Jack's.

"Here's a running bow line," he said.

He started to make it as a line of a song swam into my mind. "Throw him over board with a running bow line," I sang.

Jack didn't look up. From the wheel, I heard William belt out, "Way, hey, and up she rises." He'd raised his arm to follow the sail up the main mast.

Cooking the crew's breakfast on the stove near the stern mast, Bernard echoed in song, "Way, hey, and up she rises."

They both sang the line again, ending with "Early in the morning."

The four of us sang out the rest of the song "What do You do with a Drunken Sailor" with Bernard leading. It included not only the running bow line verse, but several others

I'd never heard before. Of course, they may have been making them up as we sailed. If I knew anything about sailing, I might have added a verse myself.

My hands moved in rhythm, creating the new knots. After I got each knot down Jack showed me another, having me do and redo them until I knew I'd be doing them in my sleep.

"So, when's the boat going to get to Alpena?"

"Boat?" Jack jerked his head up.

"Sorry. I meant that little one hanging over there," I covered quickly, although my explanation sounded stupid even to me. Jack looked to where I pointed, to the small boat latched at the bow.

"Yawl. It's called a yawl."

"All right, then," I said, "When does that yawl and this great ship, the *City of Cheektowaga,* arrive in Alpena?"

"Tomorrow afternoon, I reckon, barring any storm delays."

A day and a half to travel to Alpena. It was farther away from Dowagic than I thought.

"So do you use the *yawl* for going ashore or something?"

"Could, I suppose. It's mostly for if we, you know, and need to climb into it."

"You mean, sink?"

Jack slapped his hand over my mouth and looked around. "Take it back, boy. Take it back."

I wiggled his boney fingers from my face. "Take what back?"

"That word. Bad luck to use that word aboard."

I thought about it for a moment, and then sucked in my breath. Jack frowned. I was prepared to get slapped again.

"Backwards. Say the word backwards."

I looked up at the flapping American flag and said, "K-I-N-S."

Jack seemed surprised that I spelled it. "So say it."

"Kins."

He looked so relieved that I almost laughed.

"And what does it matter when we arrive, as long as we do, and as long as we get paid. Two wrecks, I've survived. A third one would be bad luck."

Again with the bad luck. It was my turn to roll my eyes. "I want to get myself prepared to go to the captain's sister's house."

Jack sat back on his haunches and gave me a funny look. "What stories are you telling? The captain doesn't have a sister. He's got no relations at all over here in America except that cousin, Finbarr. Who's been filling your head with such nonsense?" He squinted, turning his left side to me.

I heard the words he spoke. They floated and circled above my head just out of reach of comprehension.

"If you're trying to get in good with Captain Klaus or something, it won't work."

My stomach didn't feel well. I hadn't been seasick on this entire voyage, not yet. The more what Jack said sunk in caused my insides to threaten coming up. I rushed to the rail and leaned over. I gagged a few times, but nothing came. I turned and slid my back along the wall and sat on the deck.

"Captain's not going to like you slacking off like this," Jack said. "Nor that you're telling lies about his family."

I looked at the captain's door.

No sister? Then why was I here?

I rose to go in there and ask him just that. He might not have a sister, a fact I wasn't even certain of as yet. But I did. I had two sisters, two sisters whom I'd promised to take care of.

Maybe Jack was lying to me. Or the captain. I wasn't sure who.

I couldn't really do anything about the fact that I was on Lake Huron aiming north to our next port. Maybe I would just wait until we reached land where there wasn't the possibility about being tossed overboard in any little disagreement with liars. I could wait. I could wait until we docked in Alpena before I confronted him. After all, it might not even be necessary. Not if Jack was the liar. If Captain Klaus did have a sister in Alpena, then all this worry was for naught.

I'd wait.

I'd wait until Alpena.

Chapter Eight
A GHOST STORY

It was fair weather, so said the seasoned sailors on board, with about three to four foot waves. The loggers came topside in shifts. Several offered to help. I wondered if by doing so they were expecting to have a job aboard instead of in the woods. The ship suddenly felt small and crowded. I went down to my hammock. Bernard sat on it playing a card game facing Jack sitting on the lower hammock across the aisle, William's hammock. I started back topside when the opening to the hold beckoned. I slipped down the ladder and plopped onto a sack of flour. I rocked as one with the ship.

"Ho, Honor, me hearty. You be lookin' too cast-down-like."

Old Salty, or whatever his real name was, looked out from behind a pile of full burlap sacks.

I sniffed. "Do not. I was just thinking of my sisters, that's all." I rose and started to leave. With two people down here, even the hold was feeling crowded.

"Wanna be hearin' a ghost story to cheer ye up-like?" Old Salty offered, running his wrinkled hand through the tangle of his hair.

"Wanna be getting back up to where you belong-like?" I snapped.

Old Salty looked wide-eyed at me. Then he moaned and dropped his chin to his chest in a heavy sigh. It occurred to me that maybe Old Salty was who Chas heard moaning in this very hold so long ago. Thinking of Chas reminded me once more of Bridget and Sissy. I raised a corner of my lip and resolved not to worry about what I had no control over. I had to stop thinking about them – at least for now. This poor or stowaway probably was just lonely and wanted someone to talk to. Besides, it wouldn't hurt any to listen to the ramblings of an old man, even if he was undoubtedly a bit touched in the head.

"I'm sorry," I told him. "Sure. What ghost story do you know?"

He perked right up and settled himself on a flour sack. He pointed an open hand to a sack opposite him. I sat as he began.

"There once be this here cook-woman aboard a ship-like. Her ship made port just as a big ole northern gagger struck. But there be no more slips in the harbor, so they tied on to another schooner, which was tied to the dock. So's this cook she be thinkin' that she needs to be a'goin ashore to see about getting' supplies. But in the fury of the storm, she slips and be a'fallin' between the two schooners and crushed. Now she be a'hauntin' her old ship-like."

Old Salty stopped and squinted at me. I waited. He kept silent.

I sat back. "That's it?" I said at last. "That wasn't at all scary."

"You be tellin' me how to tell ghost stories, laddie?"

I'd offended him. "Maybe if you lower your voice and slow down your speech, it will make it sound creepier. And maybe if you added more details, like—" I pulled my head down between lifted shoulders and squinted at Old Salty, continuing his story in a cracked whisper, "And when she screamed, no one did anything to help her. They thought it be the wind screaming. So she cursed them. *Cu-u-ursed* them, I say! So today, if you happen to be aboard that very ship where the old cook died, you might see the white whisp of a woman walking from the galley and stepping over the railing. And some dark nights when you're all alone, you may even hear her screaming, screaming." My voice crept higher, "Screeeeeaming!"

Old Salty shivered. "Aye, Honor, me lad," he said. "That be a good ole tellin'. Let me be a'tryin' another for ye." He took a deep breath and let it out slowly with a low moan coming from deep within his chest. I smiled and nodded. That sound was creepy enough to get my eyes to start to water.

"Now," he said slowly looking at me through one eye. "Ye know how there be stone buildings in cities around the lakes?"

I nodded, even though I'd only been to two cities on the Great Lakes. I smacked my lips, about to inform him that wasn't a very good opening for a ghost story.

"Them stones, limestone they be called, they must come from somewhere, after all. So's a lot came from Kelly's Island ten years or so, back in the 1840's. Over there in Lake Erie-way."

"We crossed Lake Erie to get to Detroit," I said. "Did we pass near the island?" We. That meant my sisters and me. I slouched. This story was not helping me to forget them any.

"Aye, we done pass nearby. But more than nearby, laddie. We be passin' over it."

"Over an island?" I said. "How could you fly over an island?"

"Not over the island. Over the tunnel."

I settled back into my flour sack. This story was becoming more interesting.

"Ye see, it be Italian immigrants who be a'makin' up most of the miners. Good workers underground, they are. They be a'cuttin' and diggin' up all the limestone they could from Kelly's Island-like without sinking it. The ships now, they kept a'comin' to load up more of that there precious limestone. More and more, they a'be wantin'. And more and more, the owner wants to be a'givin' them. The stone, it be turnin' into money, ye see? But the limestone, now, although it be gone-like from the island, diggin' deeper, they be discoverin' it keeps on goin', goin' right under the lake."

Old Salty nodded with his lips pursed out. I nodded, too. He told this one better. However, I waited for the ghost part to come.

"The owners of the mine, now, they be a'figurin' they could be keepin' that limestone money comin' by diggin' sideways-like. So's they be makin' a tunnel right under Lake Erie, a'headin' it toward the mainland a couple miles away, and maybe right under that land over there. Then one awful day, a blast in the tunnel be explodin' too near the bottom of Lake Erie above them-like. And ye can imagine what happened next. That's right, Honor, me lad. Flooded. The tunnel, it be flooded, along with all them Italians who be a'workin' down there. It be drownin' the lot of them. Dozens of good hard-workin' men. And the worst of it is that no bodies ever be recovered-like. Bodies need to be buried, good and proper-like, or them spirits without their bodies, they be a'getting' restless, see?"

Old Salty paused.

When I figured out where he was going with his story, I felt it. A prick at the back of my neck. It started as just a little tickle. Then my hair rose as the tickle radiated outward.

50

"So's now," Old Salty whispered, "whenever there be cargo ships a'passin' overhead their tunnel, ships a'carryin' goods for greedy owners, them Italians, they be a'draggin' their chains up, up, and slippin' them over the ships-like sailin' on the surface. And pullin' them down, down, down to be avengin' their deaths-like on the greedy owners, just like the limestone mine owners who be killin' the lot of them."

I shook with a full-fledged shiver and stood. I suddenly remembered Chas complaining about hearing chains and moaning someplace over Lake Erie. I shivered again. I rubbed the goosebumps down from my arms and cleared my throat.

"Better," I told Old Salty. "But it didn't scare me in the least. It's just a little damp down here. That was the reason I, you know—"

"Aye, matie. I be knowin'," he said. He scrounged up his shoulders and raised his bushy eyebrows at me. And for a moment it really did look like his eyes glowed.

"Yeah. Well. You'd best get back to where you belong now." I turned for the ladder, wondering where the pirate expression "shiver me timbers" came from.

As if in response, the wooden sides of the boat creaked. Another chill shot down my own bones. I scurried up both ladders to get to the sunshine topside.

Chapter Nine
ALPENA

The land pulled away westward. Sea gulls flew around our masts, calling out. It seemed to me that we must be at the very tip of Michigan by now because there was nothing but water ahead of us and water to the starboard and stern, like we were dropping off the top of the world.

One of the lumberjacks shouted over the port side, "Roger! Norman! Ho there!"

"Someone fell overboard?" I gripped the railing and scanned the waves. I wondered if lumberjacks knew how to swim or if the captain who was so set on his schedule would bother to turn back for them. I didn't spot bobbing heads. We had to be too late. I pulled in a breath to shout, "Man overboard." The big man in red flannel flopped a hand on my shoulder and shook his head.

"No. No," he answered. "It's my cousins. They're over there, lumbering in Saginaw. I told them I'd give them a holler when we passed by." He waved again shouting, "Ho, Roger! Ho, Norman!"

I wanted to cry out, "Ho, Sissy! Ho, Bridget."

Oh, where was Alpena, and how big was this Lake Huron? I didn't have too long to wait. We arrived in Alpena's port at two in the afternoon, right on schedule. The immigrants and some of the corn and flour left the ship. The lumberjacks disembarked, too. They left their gear aboard ship, so I assumed they'd be returning. I kept waiting for Captain Klaus to make some indication to me about his sister. The *City of Cheektowaga* wasn't leaving until the next morning. Captain Klaus probably wanted to spend time with his sister. He gave the crew leave. Jack, Bernard and William bolted down the plank and headed for the nearest tavern.

I eyed the captain. Only Finbarr and he were on board. I approached them.

"What do you want me to do?" I asked the captain.

"Shore leave," he answered.

"I meant—" I bit my lower lip. "I meant, is there any place I should go? Or anyone I should, say, meet this evening?"

Captain Klaus put back his head and bellowed a laugh. "I think you're a bit young to be meeting up with any of the lasses here, but if that's what you want, I can tell you the most likely place to be entertained even for someone as young as you."

"I meant— No. I mean—"

"Quit your stammering, boy. Go ashore. Have fun. Just be back before dawn."

Be back before dawn? Perhaps his sister couldn't come tonight, or maybe Klaus hadn't let her know about me and wanted to break it to her first. Or maybe she couldn't come until tomorrow morning. The nagging, "if he has a sister" crept into the back of my mind. I figured it was just one more night aboard the *City of Cheektowaga* and I'd be either with a new family in Alpena or on my way to Dowagiac to be with my own, real sisters.

I hung onto the rail and closed my eyes.

Soon, I sent to my sisters.

I walked down the plank walk to the dock. After about

three steps, my legs went all wobbly beneath me and I clung onto a post. I fell to the dock as my head spun. Whoever was moving the dock, I wish they'd stop. My betraying eyes tricked me. The dock didn't look like it swayed. Only a handful of people were around, and none seemed too interested in moving the dock. The small waves barely made a sound as they lapped against the pier and ships. I knew this wasn't sea sickness. Was there such a thing as being land sick?

Laughter from the first mate drifted down from above me.

"You'll be getting your land legs back again soon," the captain said.

I quickly stood. I hadn't seen anyone else waddle down the dock before me. I forced my legs to behave and trust my eyes not to see wobbly. Step by slow step, I finally cleared the dock and stood on solid ground for the first time since Buffalo, New York. Three taverns lined the first street, along with a bank for sailors, a sail maker shop, rope makers, and food venders. Tobacco and whiskey were prevalent everywhere, both for sale and consumed on the spot. My land legs returned to me by the end of the street. I stood by a coffin maker shop, admiring the pine boxes and wishing those Italians under Lake Erie each could have their own to be buried within so they wouldn't feel the need to haunt. If I believed in such things, that is.

The further inland I went, the nicer the store fronts became. So did the houses. Yellows and greens and reds and blues trimmed with lacey white gingerbread and wrap-around porches. As beautiful as the blues and whites of the sea are, I found myself admiring these charming houses on their tree-lined streets. The maple trees had started turning colors. The reds and yellows and oranges among the houses gave the entire area a cheerful feel.

I imagined that the Captain's sister lived in one of these nicer houses. After all, her brother was a captain. That might make it worthwhile to stick around for a while before I went to check on my sisters. I'd work really hard for Captain Klaus' sister. She'd appreciate everything I did so much that she'd not only let me, but encourage me to visit my sisters to see for myself how they were doing.

My stomach growled, reminding me that I hadn't had anything to eat since lunchtime. I had no money to buy food in Alpena. If I returned to the *City of Cheektowaga*, I could probably scrounge up some food in the ship's pantry.

When I returned, dock hands using ropes and pulleys loaded barrels of something heavy aboard the ship. There were fifteen barrels which I counted, and I don't know how many had been loaded before that. Captain Klaus stood topside, supervising the procedure. I assumed that Finbarr was below deck, directing where the barrels would go. The captain followed the last man down to the lower deck. I climbed onboard and scoured the galley pantry. Stale cake and wilted carrots were all I could find. It was something to chew on and tamed my noisy stomach. I hoped Bernard wouldn't miss it. As I indulged in my supper, the barrel carriers left the ship. With my stomach now satisfied, I went below deck to the crew's quarters. No one was there. I expected none. Curiosity pulled me down the front hatch into the hold.

The sun was just setting, and without a lantern, the steerage area was pitch black. I smelled the oil and carbon from a lantern recently in the area, but still couldn't see. I started to feel around. There seemed to be more burlap bags now with only a passageway between. I felt my way along the aisle until my eyes adjusted to the dark shadows and made it down the length of the ship. Away back at the stern, behind a stack of sacks, and with more sacks piled on top of them, I found the barrels. They almost seemed intentionally hidden.

I leaned close and sniffed. I nearly choked on the smell.

"Boo!" whispered a quick voice near my ear.

I startled and nearly yelped.

"Salty! What are you still doing here?"

The old man shook with laughter. "Did I be a'scarin' ye that time, Honor?"

"No. Yes. I mean, no. Why are you here? Everyone's on shore."

"Not everyone, Honor, me lad. No, not everyone. There be the likes of you and the first mate and captain up top. And then there be the likes of me."

"You aren't one of the immigrants, are you?"

Old Salty laughed. "No. No. No, laddie."

If he wasn't a sailor or lumberjack or immigrant... My suspicion was correct. Old Salty was a stowaway! I should probably report him. Maybe I would. But the old guy wasn't causing any harm. He leaned in close over one of the barrels and took in a big sniff. Yep. He must be a stowaway, one who eats our food. That would make him a thief. If I saw him stealing our food and drink, I would have to report him for sure. I liked Old Salty. Any stowaway would probably be better off on land.

Then I remembered our New York stoop which my sisters and I shared for half a year. I couldn't kick the old man out of his home. It would be like the police making their sweeps of street kids and take them to jail. I frowned and swallowed hard. Old Salty wouldn't fare too well in a jail. Life aboard the *City of Cheektowaga* was a safe place for an old man like him. After all, he deserved to live free, too. If I were staying on, I'd cut back on my own rations so there'd be enough for him, too. But I was leaving soon.

Old Salty closed his eyes and moaned a longing moan over the barrel.

I sniffed again, too. The distinctive smell in the newly boarded barrels was, without a doubt, whiskey. No mistaking that repulsive smell. I couldn't see how anyone could stomach the retched stuff. The only thing I could figure out was maybe they drank it to take away inhibitions to talk and act silly, or give them fake courage to be mean. I'd seen enough of that back in New York, and the men and women who never remembered the cruel or ridiculous things they said or did. In either case, silly or mean, that sure seemed like a dumb reason to drink the stuff. I waited for Old Salty to break open one of the barrels and help himself. He seemed the sort who would swallow it until he forgot who he was. I tilted my head to the side, ready to stop him. Instead, he just turned and grinned away at me.

"So's. Be ye a'hankerin' for another ghost story, laddie?"

Chapter Ten
MORE STORIES

There wasn't anything else I had to do until dawn, unless I needed to report a whisky-drinking stowaway. But so far, so good.

I pulled two sacks down into the aisle, one for Salty and one for me, and we sat ourselves down.

"Ye be hearing the tale of the *Flying Dutchman*?"

I shook my head. Old Salty seemed disgusted with my lack of basic ghost story education. He sighed like a low winter wind, and settled himself back against the bags.

"The *Flying Dutchman* be about a Dutch captain of the ship *VanderDecker*. The captain, like most every captain, he be a'knowin' the importance of keepin' to a schedule and also the dangers of sailin' around Cape Horn."

"Where's Cape Horn?" I asked. "Is that near Kelly's Island?"

"Laddie, if ye keep interruptin'-like, then I be no more tellin' you tales."

"I'm sorry," I said. Maybe William would know where Cape Horn was and if we were going to pass over it, too, like Kelly Island's Tunnel. "Please continue."

"Now the sea near the Horn around Africa-like, it be moody and a'churnin'. It be allowin' ships to pass only if it likes, ye see? Well, the captain of the *VanderDecker*, now, he didn't like bein' a'tossed and a'turned about in those seas south of that there Cape Horn. He shook his fist and swore to the Almighty God that he'd be damned if he would be a givin' up tryin' to get around that there Horn."

I sucked in my breath at his foul language.

Old Salty squinted and moaned out an "Oooo."

"Ye be right in thinkin' that be a bad thing, Honor, me lad, for the *VanderDecker*, ye see, she never made port. But that *Flying Dutchman*, on the deck of his ship, he be seen here and there, sailin' and sailin', for all eternity tryin' to keep his schedule, tryin' to make his way around that Cape Horn. Sometimes the ship appears, and sometimes she disappears."

"You mean it becomes a ghost ship?"

"Aye. She be a *cursed* ghost ship, t'boot. For them ships whose sailors done seen her, why them ships themselves end up being a'cursed, too. Some be a'wreckin' up on shoals or beaches, and some be sailing down t' Davie Jones' Locker at the bottom of the deep, deep sea."

I thought about his story for a moment. He'd mentioned it was around Africa. Well, that was over on the other side of the Atlantic Ocean. I didn't need William to tell me where that was. I was a Newsie, after all. I knew where countries and continents were.

"So what you're saying is that we can't be cursed by seeing the *Flying Dutchman*, can we? Not if we're in the middle of America?"

Old Salty groaned.

"Laddie, ships can be cured for many a reason." He paused to gaze slowly around the hull. I couldn't help myself. I looked around, too. She seemed sound enough. "But there be ships that sail these Inland Seas," Old Salty continued, "who also don't be makin' port. Instead, they appear over and over to sailor folk."

"Like what?" I harbored no worries of seeing any ghost ships from down here in the hold – if I believed in such Tom-foolery.

"Now I tell ye. Once, a few years back this be, when I sailed aboard the *Flying Cloud*, one night the lookout be a'yellin' for us to swing hard to the port, as there be a schooner dead ahead of us. I be topside then and be a'witnessin'this all, mind ye. Aye.

"The wheelman, he be turnin' sharp-like, and we scraped alongside the length of that other vessel with no injuries to man or ship. I be shoutin' out as we be a'passin', shakin' my fist and yellin' at them for sailin' in the dark without no lights in either her rigging or her binnacle." He stopped and shook his head back and forth as he released air like a low whistle. "But, Honor, me lad, there be no one topside answerin' me back. When we be clearin' her, our captain, lookin' at the dark silhouette, he first be plenty angry. He was not bein' one to appreciate risk-takin' ships. Angry as he be, he be a good captain-like. So he turns us around to see if they be in need of assistance. Maybes they be all sick-like and can't be a'answerin' us, see?

"I got me into the yawl with the mate and another hand to row over and check her out. *Jamestown* was the schooner's name, clear as anything over her stern. The mate and me, we climbed aboard and commenced to a shoutin'. But no one be answerin'. She be a'missin' her yawl, though. Sure 'nough, she be a'missin' her yawl."

Salty paused to let that sink in.

So maybe the *Jamestown* crew figured the ship was sinking and abandoned ship? As if reading my mind, Old Salty continued.

"There be no leak, because I be a'checkin' her hold with every hair on the back of my neck standin' up all tall-like. Ya know that feeling, do ye, lad?"

I nodded.

He smiled and went on.

"Besides that missing yawl, everything else was in ship-shape order. The ropes, they be all coiled down-like, and every halyard be made fast as they should be. Food and plates, they all be stashed neatly in the pantry-like." He nodded. "Even t'captain and mate's coats be hangin' neatly upon a hook in the cabin.

"Well, I tell ye, Honor, we gets off that ship as quickly as we could. We be reportin' to our captain, and he be a'thinkin' we be makin' good salvage money from the abandoned ship. So we got her hawser over her bow and be tyin' her to the *Flying Cloud*. Just as that be done, and we be pullin' her along nice and gentle-like, don't ye know, a white squall came upon us. It tossed us about sos we be a'fightin' for our own souls. When things be calmin' down, I turns around and the *Jamestown*, she be gone. Her hawser line snapped in two-like."

"Did you go back to look for her?" I asked. "Did you find her or report it when you made land?"

"Nay and nay, laddie. We done recognize a black cat ship when we be seein' one. Aye. We be continuin' on-like, and tells no one, except for the few who be in taverns when we be havin' a bit more whiskey to drink than we ought." He looked at me with his dark, dark eyes. "Or we be tellin' it to young laddies who be hankerin' for a story." He slowly winked at me. "We be sailors, Honor. We like our jobs at sea. Tellin' such tales to the authorities be only makin' them a'thinkin' we be crazy-like."

I sighed long. I didn't believe in ghosts, nor in ghost ships.

Old Salty told me more tales of yet other ghost ships spotted upon the Great Lakes, until my eyes started to droop. I heard the drunken crew and lumberjacks returning aboard the *City of Cheektowaga*. I jerked my head up and popped opened my eyes. I yawned and stretched, curling my back like an old alley cat.

"Thanks, Salty. Thank you for the stories." I rose and put my flour sack back on its stack. Old Salty stood and I did the same with his.

"Nay. Thank *ye*, Honor, me lad. It does me old timbers good to be a'talkin' to a live young lad. Aye."

I nodded and yawned once more.

"Good night, Salty."

I climbed up the ladder to go to my hammock. Sleep was sweeping over me in waves.

Live young lad?

Chapter Eleven
ALPENA ASTERN

Naturally, I woke before dawn, the time when we were to set sail. I didn't bother putting on William's old sea boots. I wouldn't be needing them where I was going. I pulled on my old shoes. Both laces broke again.

I probably won't even need these any more, I thought. I'd let my dear new parents buy me a new pair. They couldn't help but want to do so when they discovered me barefoot, especially when Captain Klaus' sister hears how her brother gave my new pair away to those poor immigrants, along with my suitcase. I bet she lived in one of the large houses overlooking Lake Huron, one where she could keep a watch for her brother's brief visits. I hoped they had good family time together last night.

Family. I didn't even think to ask if there were other children in his sister's family.

I would do everything she asked of me, until I could visit my own sisters in Dowagiac. Reverend Brace back in New York wouldn't appreciate my plan very much. The first part, yes. The second part, no. His Newsboys Lodging House was for runaways. He wanted his runaways to find stable families with which to live. Hopefully, Sissy and Bridget's new family, when I found them, would be willing to take in a strong sailor boy who knew how to tie knots and swab the decks. I successfully did not gag when I thought of that last bit.

I went topside and tossed my old shoes overboard. Nothing was holding me back now from my new life. I searched the streets for the captain's kind-looking sister. The sky was dawning behind me, in the east. The streets were vacant except for the dock hands who were untying our lines. It wasn't until Jack and Bernard started pulling the lines up onto deck that I realized we were embarking.

I scrambled up the ladder to the wheel.

"Captain Klaus," I panted. "What about your sister?"

He didn't look at me. The bushy-faced first mate pushed me aside with a "Go help Jack with the lines, Honor."

Help Jack?

I scanned the dock and streets for an older woman who would look like Captain Klaus, and wanted to have a son to help her do things about her house in Alpena.

I looked forward to the bow and found Jack.

Mr. Finbarr gave me an encouraging push on my back.

"But—," I started to protest.

The captain didn't look at me. Wouldn't look at me.

I glanced once more to the shore as I caught Bernard setting and tying the plankwalk next to the rail.

Why were we leaving the dock while I was still aboard?

As the reality of what was happing sunk in, I stared back at the captain with opened mouth. My insides felt jumbled up.

"You don't have a sister, do you?" I spit at him.

Bushy Captain Klaus ignored me as if I hadn't said a word. He glanced before and aft as the tug pulled us away from the dock.

It wasn't too late to jump ship. I could dive over the railing and hit the dock running. Maybe I'd only break a bone or two, but I'd keep on running all the way to Dowagiac.

Finbarr grabbed my arm and swung me to face him.

"Honor, I said to go help Jack. You said you were willing to help us. Are you a liar?"

Liar? I now knew who the liar was. I squinted at that captain who didn't have any sister.

Even after what he'd done to me, he still refused to look me in the eye. The mate's grip on my arm tightened until it hurt so much I knew there'd be a bruise. I started seeing black around the edges of my eyesight. It hurt, but not half of the pain storming inside my chest. I jerked my arm out of Finbarr's hold.

"Yes, sir," I mumbled sarcastically. Neither Finbarr nor Klaus were gentlemen or people of honor.

I turned to bolt over the rail. The tug had pulled our ship too far from the dock. That distance wouldn't have mattered much if I knew how to swim. I wanted to cry out: *Betrayed! Argh, me hearties! I be betrayed!*

I glared at the captain as I slid down the ladder and made my way forward to Jack.

He grinned at me and wiggled his skinny eyebrows. "Told you," he said as he neatly coiled the rope.

I hated Klaus more than I did my own mother. I hated Finbarr, too, since he knew the truth all along. I even hated Jack because he was so smug about knowing.

I helped Jack coil the ropes, wishing, instead, that I could tie them all up with it. I watched Alpena and my hope get smaller and smaller.

Well, then. I decided I'd jump ship at the next place we docked, just like smart Harold had done back in Detroit. I wondered if he'd been kidnapped as well. Now I understood why he'd done it, deserting like that. It occurred to me that I hadn't seen William this morning. Even one day aboard this ship without William to be a buffer would make for a torturous journey.

"Did William jump ship?" I choked out. I hadn't seen him since he trotted off up the streets of Alpena the evening before. I wouldn't have blamed him for leaving. I knew how he felt.

"Nope," Jack stated. "The rich boy is in the hold, ready to man the pumps."

Rich boy? I hadn't realized he was rich.

I looked at the open hatch, and then out to sea. The harbor was all smooth water, not even a single white cap. I didn't see any reason to man any pumps. I wondered if people were lying to me again. I wondered if William was even on board. As I didn't see any new crew member so far, I could only believe Jack and assume William was below.

I squinted back at the captain. He didn't seem to mind what I thought, how I felt. Didn't matter. It would only be one more day before we dropped off the lumberjacks and immigrants and any of the cargo. Yes, I would leave right along with them. I'd slip among the crowd and then run so fast that not even First Mate Finbarr would be able to catch me. I'd disappear in the woods until the *City of Cheektowaga* heaved away. And good riddance. It was a bad luck ship.

The tug pulled away from us and we sailed eastward, climbing and descending small swells which quickly grew to fairly high ones. Then sailing down at a steep angle to the bottom of the wave valleys. I thought about the forty-seven of us New York street urchins and how sick the others had been back on Lake Erie. That lake was a cake walk compared to what we were going through now. Bridget and Sissy would have screamed down in the dark hold. Without seeing the waves coming, I might have screamed, too.

We were close to land, but within those watery valleys, all you could see around you was the sea, our tiny ship, and a spot of cloudy skies directly overhead.

Captain Klaus remained at the wheel.

"There are some dangerous shoals to avoid before we head north once more," Jack enlightened me.

There were some small islands I could see when we were on top of the swells. But shoals and shallow rocks just below the sea's surface? Those hidden rocks or shallow places were hard to spot. Impossible to spot. You just had to know where they were, or paid close attention to the charts. Jack said this was Klaus' thirteenth trip past Alpena, so he ought to know what's there and what's not.

Apparently, the captain of another schooner didn't have this same knowledge. At the top of each wave, I saw her stranded as waves washed over her deck. She wasn't sinking because she was obviously hung up on a shoal. Lake Huron bashed her about a bit. Her crew moved quickly about the deck, latching the sheets and I was certain, manning the pump. A wave knocked down a man. I reached out as though the action of my outstretched hand could keep him from going overboard. He stood right up and continued pulling at the lines.

The *City of Cheektowaga* sailed right past them.

"Aren't we going to help?" I asked.

"If they wanted help, they'd of signaled us," Jack answered.

They were so busy trying to stay afloat that I'm not sure they were even aware of us. A steamer followed us out of port. Maybe they'd stop to help.

"If they're damaged, they'll just head back to Alpena for repairs," Jack mentioned so casually as though a ship in distress wasn't actually in distress.

I thought how one of those light towers would be a good thing to have along this Thunder Bay. It would warn off ships from scraping the shoals and breaking up.

By the time I thought we'd crossed east right over Lake Huron and be able to see Canada at any swell top, Lake Huron calmed to gentle seven foot swells. The captain swung around, giving the helm to Finbarr, and we headed north once again. Klaus might have a character made of horse manure, but I was glad enough that he was in charge of charting our way through this dangerous area.

By lunchtime, when First Mate Finbarr assigned my four- and two-hour shifts, I realized I was an official crew member. I wasn't really in a position to argue. If I protested, I could be sent overboard.

After supper I had free time before my four hour watch. Four hours on. Four hours off. And two two-hour shifts. I knew I should rest, so lay in my hammock a while, swaying with the waves. The passengers were having a rough time of it as we pitched with each wave. I knew I would be assigned deck swabbing duty again whenever we made port, wherever that would be. But I wouldn't be aboard long enough for that. I'd slip away, I would. Argh.

Chapter Twelve
SHIFTS

When my watch was over I climbed into the empty hold, my closest feeling of home aboard this ship. I leaned against the damp hull, feeling a different sort of dampness spring to my eyes.

"I wish I hadn't let Sissy talk me into coming to Michigan," I muttered into the shadows. "What has it gotten us? Are we any better off for it? I can't even write to them because I don't know who they are with."

I heard someone sniff, and not in a sad sort of way.

"Hello?" I said into the darkness.

"Your sisters, your sisters, your sisters. All you think about is your sisters."

It was Old Salty. He hadn't abandoned ship after all.

"Yes, I do," I admitted. "And do you want to know why? Because I'm their big brother. That's why. Because I'm responsible for them. Because I don't know if they're happy or even alive. If I just knew something about them, it would be different. But I don't. You obviously don't have any family or anyone you care about, Salty."

I crossed my arms and slammed them against my ribs, turning my back on him. The tension in the room was thick enough to slice with a bow knot, and I didn't care. The old fool. He had no idea what I was going through. Why did I even bother to come down here?

"Be ye wantin' another—"

A shadow blackened the hatch as someone came down. It brightened up with a lantern held out at arm's length. Finbarr's eyes met mine. He gazed over to where the lone barrel sat.

"Just what do you think you're doing down here?"

"Talking!" I spit back. I'd probably get into more trouble for talking to the first mate like that, but I was still mad at Old Salty, mad at Klaus, mad at the world. My anger had overflowed to the tricky first mate.

"Talking to yourself?" Finbarr said.

I turned to discover that cowardly Salty had hidden himself away in the shadows.

Finbarr continued down to the hold and shook his index finger at me. "You're not allowed down here. No reason to be here. Get out!"

I rose and took a step towards him. He slapped me on the side of my head and my ear rang.

"You been getting into the supplies any? Been sneaking drinks down here, haven't you?"

"No!" My anger at his ridiculous accusation made me sound defensive. I hadn't done anything wrong. He could ask Old Salty if he wanted. If he could find the slippery guy. I wouldn't touch that poison whiskey even if it tasted like sweet fall apple cider. I put my hand on the ladder.

Finbarr squinted at me. "You know what we do with worthless or drunk crew members, don't you?"

"Make them walk the plank?" I knew that was the wrong answer before I saw the look of surprise on his face, accompanied by another head slap which I hadn't seen coming quickly enough to avoid.

"We throw them overboard with a running bowline or drag them right along the keel." His open palm motioned from the bow to the stern.

I followed his hand. I could probably hold my breath that long, as long as I had the rope to hang onto to get back into the ship. I scurried up the ladder to the next deck, then up the next. Bernard was at the wheel now. I was exploding with angry energy. I needed to run. Without thinking about what I was doing, my fast-beating heart urged me on. I scrambled up the ratlines to the cross bar at the top of the mast. It was the first time I'd been so inspired to make it all the way up there. I clung to the mast and hoped Finbarr wouldn't find me for a while. Maybe for a moment, if he came looking, he'd think I jumped overboard or something. Serve him right to worry. Although, I really don't think he was the worrying kind.

Up on the mast, the ship's sway was more noticeable than on deck. I allowed my spine and head to sway to the ship's movement. The horizon popped up on my left and disappeared. It then popped up on my right, and disappeared. And back to the left.

My stomach started feeling funny.

Me? I never got seasick.

Then I vomited. The bile splashed into the sea when we tipped that way.

I felt a little better, but waited until my stomach calmed before slithering down the ratlines and into my hammock where the swaying motion was much gentler.

When two bells struck, I struggled to put on my heavy sea boots, although I didn't really know if they were mine or not. I went topside with Bernard who hadn't mentioned my incident to the captain. Captain Klaus and William went below for their beds.

The *City of Cheektowaga's* lantern hung high by the wheel. There was another in the rigging to allow others to see us and one on the bow. Another ship heading northbound appeared and disappeared in the waves about a quarter of a mile ahead of us, and far behind us two others sailed the shipping lane.

The sky above held more stars than I'd ever seen in my life. With the dark new moon, they stretched from horizon to horizon. Back in New York, we were mostly inside after dark, except when Mother tossed us to the street. Then, we were surrounded by buildings and only saw the few stars in a patch directly overhead. Here, in the middle of Lake Huron, night was an entirely different world. I could see the Big Dipper, of course. My father used to talk about how people could find their way by it. I didn't know any other constellations, and I didn't know how to use anything but roads to find my way to Dowagiac. The stars in the Milky Way sat so close together that it looked like a roadway through the sky.

My boots gripped the wooden deck. If I were barefoot now, I'd be sliding, perhaps even sliding right over the railing.

There wasn't much to do during this watch, except to look out for other ships or debris or watch the sky. I hoped I'd catch sight of the *Jamestown*. I grinned at the thought.

Another schooner passed in the night. We were close enough to speak, but I merely waved, unwilling to break the silence of the crystal night with friendly shouting.

The rocking waves caused me to get drowsy. I knew if I nodded off while I stood by the rail, there was a good chance I'd tumble right into the sea. I slapped my face a couple times. It only stung. I couldn't keep that up for the rest of my shift. I eyed Bernard at the wheel and felt my heart race. It was just him and me on this part of the night shift. I was suddenly awake. I meandered back to the stern and nodded. Bernard looked at me, but otherwise didn't respond. At least he didn't shout at or shove me away. Just approaching the beast had me wide awake.

"So, how long have you been sailing?" I ventured.

"Always," he grunted, his large hands firmly casually holding the wheel.

He'd answered without getting mad at me. I found it encouraging.

"Where you from?" I asked.

"Don't remember."

"Where's your family?"

"Don't care."

How could someone not care about his family?

When I opened my mouth to ask another question, he jerked his head at m. The sides of his mustache framed his mouth like stage curtains. I snapped my mouth shut. It was the most conversation we'd shared this trip. I nodded at him and walked back to the bow.

I closed my eyes as the wind pushed my hair forward. The hardest thing about sailing at night was staying awake. The cold October wind teased me with water sprays. When I opened my eyes Old Salty stood not two inches from my face.

I sucked in my breath and nearly screamed.

He rounded his shoulders and squinted at me, the wind hardly moving his hair at all. "Did I be a'scarin' ye that time, Honor lad?"

"Yes, you did," I admitted, and frowned. "You startled me."

"Argh. Be it startlin' now?" He shook his head and looked sadly down to the deck. "Startlin' ain't quite the same as a'scarin'. No it ain't."

I almost laughed at his disappointed look.

"All right then," I told him. "You scared me."

He squinted at me again and muttered an "Argh." I clasped my folded hands to my chin and shivered. He stood up straight.

"You be a'pullin' me leg, laddie."

"Sorry, but shouldn't you be below deck?"

"Wells now, I be havin' pretty much free walkin' aboard this here ship."

Who was I to argue? I looked into the night and watched the northbound ship ahead of us appear and disappear.

"And speakin' of leg-pullin', did I be tellin' ye about Peg Leg Bill?"

I shook my head. It sounded like a pirate's tale. I wrapped my right arm around the bow line and settled against the railing for a story. As long as I kept an eye out for dangers, I figured I could be a'listenin' to Old Salty, too.

"Well, seems this man done lost his leg whilst a captain in the War of 1812," Old Salty started. "T'weren't much he could be a'doin' after that, like farmin' or minin' with only one leg. But he be a'likin' the sea. Oh, yes, he be a'likin' the sea. So he becomes a merchant ship captain-like, and that suited him just fine. Suited his wife and son, too, for, aye, it be good pay an' there be no more whinin' and complainin' about earnin' his keep. One day, Ole Peg Leg Bill, his ship be late in reaching port. Days they be a'passin' and there be no word of what happened, not even bits of the ship-like driftin' to shore. She just fell into a crack in the sea, with cargo and man alike."

Old Salty paused. I turned to him. "That can't be the end of the story," I said.

He moaned long and low. I don't know how he held his breath so long like that.

"Noooo," he said in another moan. "The end of Peg Leg Bill? Why, yes. The end of the story? Oh, no. It be weeks later when that wooden leg of Bill's be a'floatin' up on shore rights near the town where the wife and son be living. But there be no body with it. Just the wooden leg. There be no mistakin' whose leg it be." Old Salty nodded.

"Peg Leg Bill's," we said at the same time.

"Sure 'nough."

"How did they know it was his?" I asked. "Surely there are others who've sailed these lakes with a peg leg."

"Aye, matie, there be that. Smart lad, Honor. But how many wooden legs be havin' Peg Leg Bill's name carved right into it, eh?"

"And it floated right to his family's shore?"

"Aye."

I shivered.

Salty grinned satisfactorily before taking in a big inhale. The sail above us flapped and then refilled with air, as if it, too, was breathing.

"Be ye wantin' another. I know other tales, matie. Argh, I do be knowin' other tales."

I shrugged, but I really wanted him to go on.

"Be I tellin' ye of the first mate named Louis who didn't be believin' in banks?"

"You mean he didn't believe they existed?" I asked. "Or he didn't trust his money in them?"

Old Salty squinted hard at me.

"Sorry for interrupting. Please continue."

"One November, this Louis aboard the schooner *Garibaldi,* he be keepin' himself a money belt. He also be keepin' more money stashed up-like in his mattress, too. During a gale on old Ontario, they couldn't reach a port's shelter, but they got themselves near. They be droppin' their hook overboard to hold them steady, figurin' to wait out the storm while they pumped her hold."

I thought of the water in our own hold and although I didn't know where this story was heading, I had a sudden desire to go down and do some pumping of my own.

"Didn't take them long," Salty continued, "before they realized their anchor be slippin'-like along the bottom, and the gale be pushin' the *Garibaldi* towards a sandbar. All the men climbs into the yawl, all except Louis. He be stayin' with his money, see?"

I stretched and yawned. "So Louis drowned along with his money belt and mattress."

"Noooo," moaned Old Salty. He glared until I swear he made his eyes look almost red.

I slapped a hand over my mouth. "Continue," I muttered into my hand.

"The next morning, there be some ner-do-well men who rowed out in the stormy sea and found Louis standing knee-deep in the cabin, all frozen to death. They be cuttin' off his belt and skedaddlin' out of there quick-like. That afternoon, the rescue boat arrived to be findin' Louis dead frozen. They took his body to bury it, but didn't be findin' his money. Because it be a'missin'. Now a days that Louis, he be wanderin' the shore where his ship be beached, crying, "Where's my money? Where's my money?""

"Poor guy," I said. I'd be jumping ship at next port, so it didn't look like I'd ever be in need of any money belt. "Did they catch the thieves?"

"No, they be long dead by now, laddie. Long dead."

I wondered what I'd ever do if I had a lot of money. First, it would have to be honestly mine. I'm no thief. Second, maybe I'd buy a house for Sissy and Bridget and me overlooking one of the Great Lakes. I wondered if I could buy a mother.

When my four hour shift was over, I fell into my hammock fully clothed and booted.

I dreamed we were in a gale, a real gagger, as Old Salty would say. I was the captain and the wild wind tipped the *Garibaldi* – or was it the *City of Cheektowaga?* – onto her side. A big wave tossed me into the drink. I sank deeper and deeper until someone grabbed me and shook. I held my breath as he kept pulling at me. When I couldn't hold it any longer I sucked in.

You *can* breathe water!

"Wake up, you lazy lug!" Jack said, still shaking me awake. "We're in port."

Chapter Thirteen
DRUMMOND ISLAND

We'd dropped anchor off shore sometime in the early morning. By the time I came topside, the sails were already lowered and William was tying them down. A cold wind greeted me. I thought I'd gone to sleep in the late fall and awoken to mid-winter. When I came through the hatch a man on a tug tossed us a line and Bernard tossed back our bow line. Gulls circled and cried above us. A single lumberman stood watch over the operation. The smell of pine drifted over the water. The land curved away from Lake Huron. I knew we were dropping of the lumberjacks. The land before me held a lot of timber for them to harvest.

I glanced around to make sure I knew where each crew member was so I could make my get-away at the most opportune moment. William and Jack were in the bow. Bernard was mid ship. I couldn't find Finbarr. Maybe he'd jumped onto the tug. Captain Klaus called me back to help with the stern line.

I'd make my escape. Soon be off this black cat of a ship and run all the way to Dowagiac.

Two ships in full sail left port, both low in the water, their decks heavily loaded with timber. Their departure meant room for us to get to the dock to unload our own cargo and passengers. And to unload me!

The tug which had towed out the two ships now pulled us in. When we neared the dock, the tug released the lines and came around to our port side to push us against the dock. Dockhands waited for our lines. Jack trotted up to the stern where he tossed the rope to them and they secured the lines to huge pilings. Bernard did the same in the bow.

Soon.

A light frost covered the roofs and the logs waiting to be loaded. Running to Dowagiac would keep me toasty.

The topside lumberman must have signaled our passengers to disembark, for we'd barely tied off before the rest of the lumbermen pushed the plank walk off the companion way and clambered off. First mate Finbarr led the way. He walked with purpose down to the wharf. I'd have to be sure to keep an eye out for him when I made my escape. The lumberjacks disembarked after him, headed off at a quick pace to get at those trees. I knew what they felt like. The captain had me tucked up in the stern with Jack and him. After the lumberjacks, the immigrant families followed more slowly, carrying four times the amount of luggage – probably everything they owned. It was a whole lot more than I owned. Then again, even the lumberjacks had more than I did. I looked to see if I could find my suitcase among them. It was not. Watching them caused a longing rumbling inside me for my own family. I slipped away from the captain and checked ropes, getting closer and closer to the immigrants.

"I hope this island has a doctor," panted a pregnant woman on the plank below me. She held onto the hand of a toddler. She looked about ready to keel over. "At least a midwife. And soon, Peter, soon."

Soon, Honor, soon, I thought.

I didn't hear her husband's answer. A coldness at her speech flooded through me. I turned to Jack who had made his way forward to me. "This is an island?"

"A fairly good sized one," he answered.

I scanned around. How would I get to the mainland from an island? I glanced to our lying captain who'd just wanted me as an extra crew hand on board his ship. His stare back penetrated to the rear of my skull. I turned away.

"So, how far's the mainland from here?" I whispered, not that the captain would hear me. At least I didn't think he could.

Jack sniffed and squinted around him as if he could smell the answer. He nodded out to sea. "A few miles down south there, I reckon." He sent a spit of tobacco over the railing.

I looked, but Lake Huron only revealed water. I swallowed hard. "So, when do we stop on the mainland again?"

"Not till we reach Milwaukee," Jack grunted.

"And where in Michigan is that?" I asked.

Jack laughed and choked on his tobacco wad. A drool of the black juice ran down his chin. He didn't bother to wipe it away.

"Hey, William!" he shouted up to the bowswain chair. "Your boy here thinks Milwaukee's in Michigan."

William secured the sail to the mast.

"It's in Wisconsin," William shouted down. "My home state, you know." He looked out to sea as if he longed to be someplace else, too.

"Sees," started Jack up, "the captain don't want any more crew abandoning ship. If we land on the mainland, it's too easy for someone to slip off, like Harold." He spit again. "Can't sail with an inade- inade- inadequate crew."

Captain Klaus couldn't really have planned that. This port was one of the stops originally planned on this trip. Jack couldn't have known I wanted to slip off. Was I so obvious?

I wondered how far apart Milwaukee was from Dowagaic. My escape was delayed. Only delayed.

I assumed there'd be some cleaning to do aboard the *City of Cheektowaga*, like in Detroit and Alpena, and then we'd take some shore leave. Maybe I'd stay off, anyway, and stowaway on an outgoing ship. It would just be my luck to get on a ship heading upbound to Lake Superior.

It turned out we didn't get shore leave.

As soon as our passengers cleared the plank walk, Finbarr returned and oversaw us hauling out our bags of flour and barrels of whiskey. I was in the steerage with Bernard. I figured my head would stay on my shoulders as long as I was quiet, although Bernard seemed on edge.

"My family's dead," Bernard said.

I wasn't sure how to respond to that, so I said nothing.

"Died in a fire, so tell them hello."

I bit my lips together and stared at him.

He looked at me as if he noticed me with him there for the first time. "Oh." He frowned. "Harold looked like my boy."

I opened my mouth to say something, but my brain could think of nothing, so I just nodded.

I looked around for Old Salty, but couldn't find him. Maybe he'd decided to follow my plan and abandon ship, too. He didn't even say good-bye. I had to admit I was jealous. If he would have told me, I could have sneaked off with him. I silently wished him well.

Finbarr shouted through the hatch for us to leave one barrel there. We climbed up top.

Two teams of waiting horses pulled two wagonloads of

planked wood alongside our ship. Several dock hands helped load it down the hatch and into the second deck level where the animals and then the immigrants used to be. The horse team went back down the dock. Their driver unhitched the empty wagon and hitched up another one filled with large squared white pine. It took a while to get those horses in motion. The driver came to the side of our ship. There were two other wagonloads waiting on land. Between our ship's crew and about a dozen men from shore and lots of ropes and pulleys, we unloaded some of the wood onto the top deck on the starboard side until we listed nearly ten degrees. I held onto the railing, figuring we were going to roll right over and capsize at the dock. We didn't.

The waiting tug pulled us around so when we loaded the starboard side, we balanced out. And then we hauled up some more lumber causing us to list once again. I kept looking at the captain, wondering if he really knew what he was doing or not. I'd known about ships tipping over while still tied up at the dock. People died in those capsizes. I hoped we wouldn't be one of those statistics. I couldn't swim to safety. I eyed the mast. Perhaps if I climbed the mast and lashed myself to it, it would probably land on the dock or float until someone rescued me.

The tug swung around again. We loaded until we sat much lower in the water than we did with the coal and animals, and certainly lower than with just passengers and food and whiskey.

Captain Klaus seemed reluctant to stop loading. The boom barely cleared the timber we had aboard.

Before any of us crew set foot on land, dock hand threw back our lines and the tug pulled the *City of Cheektowaga* out of the harbor.

My opportunity was gone.

I neatly coiled the stern rope nice and shipshape. I helped Jack and William and Bernard hoist the sails. William started a sea tune to the rhythm of the pulls. Bernard had to take over the song since we couldn't keep William's beat. As the tug released us a light breeze softly filled the sails.

"Maybe it's because of our heavier cargo," I said.

Jack laughed. "Hey, Bernard. Did ya hear what our young Honor said?"

Soon everyone, even William, was laughing at me. I wasn't even sure why. I wanted to hide, but where could I go on this small ship? Maybe down into the hold. If I did that, then the captain and crew would think I was a coward as well as stupid. Besides, Salty was gone.

I remained topside. I leaned over the rail watching the sun dance on the water. The October breeze made me long for a jacket.

When we were about five miles out, which took us two slow hours, the wind died. The sails didn't even flap.

Chapter Fourteen
OFFSHORE

"Now what?" I asked Jack.

"We wait for something to come along to push this old wind-wagon," he answered.

I searched for a tug until I realized the something he meant was wind. Our American flag hung as limp and motionless as a wet hankie on a hook inside a house. I had the sudden urge to climb to the top and look out at this unusually calm sea and island and other stranded sailing vessels sitting in the water. My stomach became queasy reminding me of the last time I was up there.

A mechanical chugging sounded over the water and someone blasted a horn. A steamer passed by right through the still sea, out from Drummond Island. There was no need to worry about wind power with a power ship like that. Seeing them move so easily without depending on wind, I had no doubt those engine ships would be the wave of the future in sailing without sails.

Someone continued blasting on their horn. I thought we might ring our bell back at them to be all friendly-like. No one on the *City of Cheektowaga* made the move to do so. We watched as passengers and crew of the passing steamer stood at the railing, hooting and waving. "What's the matter? Run out of steam?" they shouted, or simply or simply a mocking, "Bye-bye, slowpoke."

"Ignore them," the captain said.

I wasn't sure if it was a command or not. We turned our backs on them.

They shouted over the noisy engine. Both voice and motor sounds carried easily over the calm sea. It may be the wave of the future, but it was a noisy wave. I couldn't imagine trying to sleep aboard such a noisy vessel. I was thankful for a hammock and the gentle rocking of the seas. I wished it would start rocking now some so we could get moving.

We weren't, however, the only sailing ship sitting helplessly in the sea lane. Several sailing ships sat in sight. Steamers continued moving in both directions. Moving was the important word. Moving or becalmed, this was a busy shipping lane, as busy as around Lake St. Claire and the river. I could make out the gray line of land to the west going between the upper and lower peninsulas. The lower peninsula. That would be the mainland where my sisters lived.

The passing steamers amused meat first, but soon became annoying. I spent the next couple hours pacing the deck around and over the timber while William and Jack rested below.

Bernard fixed us pancakes, and four of us sat crosslegged on deck eating. The captain and Finbarr took their food to eat in the captain's cabin, as usual.

"Lucky we're heading downbound to Milwaukee and not up to Lake Superior," Bernard said.

"Mmm?" I muttered with my mouth full of pancake.

"You're welcome." He smiled at me. The man actually knew how to smile.

I finished swallowing. "No, I meant—I mean, delicious."

I waited a bit before continuing my original question. "What's up in Lake Superior?" *Besides being even farther away from my sisters.*

"Copper and ore," Bernard replied.

"That's not the problem," Jack added. "Those rocks will last forever. The trick is pulling ships around the rapids to get to it."

"They're digging a ditch," William added.

"Rapids? A ditch?" My mind raced.

"A canal with locks to avoid the rushing rapids," William answered. He was a good teacher.

"Like on the Erie Canal?" I asked.

"Yeah," Bernard grunted. "Only now it will take a lot longer to come down through to Lake Huron."

"But safer," William added. "Lots of captains don't bother going up there. They only accept cargos down below here. It's a twenty-five foot drop between Lake Superior and Lake Huron , you know. A fast drop in a very short time."

"It's an odd name," I pointed out. "After the Sioux Indians, I suppose."

"The French explorer, LaSalle, named that stretch 'Sault Sainte Marie,'" William added. "After their Virgin Mother Mary."

"So the Sault part is after the Indian tribe, right?" William shrugged.

"Rapids," Jack repeated. "It's Indian for 'fast water' or…"

"Rapids," we all said together.

. Bernard smiled again. He wore it well. "I know something Indian about Lake Superior. There's a giant fish up in those waters, big enough to hold an entire village in its mouth."

"That's just folktales," Jack said, putting a plug of tobacco in his cheek. "I do know that there are real monsters in these lakes. One night in a tavern, a sailor told me how he'd seen one with his very eyes."

"There are no monsters," I said. "That's like believing in ghosts."

They all turned slowly to me and stared, like I'd just uttered a curse. I bit my lips together.

"As I was saying," Jack went on, "This feller says he'd seen as critter about four hundred yards off his port. Not just him, either. There were others who saw it, too. It was all brown and snake-like. About fifty foot long. It had a double row of fins along its side, and whiskers on its ugly puss."

I released a nervous laugh. "I'm sorry, but that's just plain silly. It's not even dark to be telling stories like that."

"I heard of those," William said.

"Sure you have," Bernard agreed. "Everyone's heard tell of those type of critters in these lakes."

I looked at them from face to face. They didn't seem to be pulling my leg. If they were, they were all in on it. They could believe in make-believe stories if they wanted. I wouldn't believe any sea serpents living in the Great Lakes unless I saw one for myself. We were silent for a long time.

"Life is like a sea voyage," Bernard said out of the blue. "A ship handed out to the mercy of water."

His insight surprised me.

"And traveling along knowing where the rocks and shoals are in order to avoid them," William continued.

"How about life tossing storms at your ship?" Jack added. "Big waves or hurricane winds."

I looked at our limp flag, wondering if I'd ever see my sisters again. "Or sometimes sitting becalmed, waiting," I whispered.

A splash came from our port side.

"We've got company," Bernard said.

A chill shook down my spine. I jumped to the railing, expecting to spy one of the lake monsters. I both wanted to see the wonder of the beast and was terrified of fainting .

Something long and thin glided towards us.

"Ahoy, *City of Cheektowaggy*."

Monsters speak?

The long object had ores, and many small heads, human heads. It was a yawl with three men and a woman coming from the direction of the neighboring schooner.

Klaus and Finbarr emerged from the cabin.

"Stupid," Klaus muttered.

"Ahoy on board!" the woman said from the yawl.

"Ahoy," I shouted back.

"It's *Cheektowaga*," Finbarr corrected.

I felt my cheeks flush. I should have been more defensive about our ship's name. We threw down a jack ladder and the four climbed aboard. It was embarrassing how everyone rushed to help the woman in her blue hoop skirt over the rail like she was all helpless. But her sure footholds assured me that she knew her way around a ship.

"Not much to do at the moment," said the shortest of the three men. "So we thought we'd come by for a visit." He held out a deck of cards and the mood among our crew suddenly heightened to interest. We sat in a large circle, and Shorty stared dealing. "Five card stud," he said.

The largest man among them, a man who put Bernard to shame in size and hearth, passed around a flask. We all took a swig except for Captain Klaus and Finbarr. I wasn't certain what was in the flask, but I guessed. I wasn't a captain or a first mate.

I felt obligated to take a sip. The Devil's liquid barely touched my tongue before I coughed. The others laughed. It was one thing for the men to laugh at me. I didn't like it when the woman did. The big sailor slapped my back and I nearly fell over onto the cards.

Jack passed around his tin of tobacco, but only one of the visitors took a pinch.

"So where do you folks hail from?" started the short man, looking at his cards.

"New York," Finbarr answered.

"Me, too." I spun to Finbarr. I didn't realize he came from there.

"Wisconsin," William said proudly.

"Nowhere," said Bernard with a shrug.

"Everywhere," Jack answered.

People nodded.

"We're Michigan," the woman said. "The lot of us hail from all parts of Michigan."

"Mostly Detroit," Shorty added. "So, a nickel a point?"

A nickel? I had no money. None. I wasn't even sure how to play the card game.

The flag flapped. We all jerked our necks to look upward at the breeze.

"Got to go!" the woman said. Several pairs of hands offered to help her rise.

The breeze increased to billow our mainsail. We lurched forward.

Shorty snatched up the cards, and the four of them clambered down the jack ladder and rowed like men possessed to reach their own ship before it sailed off without them.

"Stupid," reiterated Klaus.

Chapter Fifteen
BETWEEN THE PENINSULAS

We tacked to the light southwest wind to between the Lower Peninsula and Upper Peninsula. The captain was at the helm now, for he'd navigated the way through on many trips. Apparently, the reefs and rocks and small islands in the area have claimed many ships and even more lives. I hated our lying captain, but trusted his sailing knowledge. Old Salty was sure to have stories to tell about this spot.

"I could swim faster than this," I muttered, "if I knew how."

"Swim?" Bernard replied. I didn't know he was nearby. "Where are your fins? The Good Lord didn't make people to swim. You're not a fish."

"On hot summer days in New York, people went to the shore and bathed," I protested.

"Land loving cowards," Bernard said. "Ever see people venture from the shore without a line attached to their little bathing machines? This here's my life line." He grabbed a rope. "And this ship is my shore. Now get away from me."

I wandered to the bow. Still, I would think knowing how to swim might come in handy on these lakes.

As we sailed past Mackinac Island with its big white fort

up on the hill, the wind finally picked up in gusts, making it easier for us sailing ships to maneuver in the narrow shipping lane.

"That island's not even four square miles big, but the fort has switched hands several times." It was William again, spouting off his knowledge. "It was built by the British. Taken over by Americans. Retaken by the British. Given back to us Americans. And that doesn't count the various Indian tribes who lived on it before the French."

All that fuss over a tiny island. It was, I had to admit, a strategic spot for warring nations. But could anyone truly could own land?

Clouds billowed threateningly before us. I turned to go below and rest before my next duty shift.

"Now there's a light I'll be glad to have to my back," he said, grinning broadly. "From here we head southwest. Nothing but Lake Michigan ahead of us." He waved his extended hand indicating everything in one-hundred-and-eighty degrees in front of us.

My heart thumped within me. South? Like south towards Dowagaic? I glanced to the lower peninsula. It felt like years since I'd been separated from my sisters. It had only been days.

I'm coming, I sent to them over the sea.

The brown lighthouse tower William mentioned stuck out of the water, build up from the bottom of the lake. I figured it had to be very shallow over there, which was why there was need of a light. I wondered how many ships struck those rocks before they built a light to warn them away.

"It's called the Waugoshance Light," William continued, "here on the western edge of the Straights of Mackinac. Until three years ago, guess what was there instead of that tower?"

"A rock?" I answered with a chuckle.

"No," he answered. "I mean, yes, of course, there was rock, but right next to the rock was a light ship."

"A light ship?" I imagined a ship floating in the sky, anchored to the rocks so it wouldn't drift away. Or perhaps a cargo ship filled with goose down feathers.

"It's a wooden ship with a tall-tall mast and a light atop," he answered. "It was anchored in place over the reef to warn others away."

I watched the storm surge batter the tower. "Wouldn't any storm blow a light ship away?" I asked.

William looked his look at me. "Guess that's why they decided to build a lighthouse."

"Tower," I corrected. "And why are you glad to have it behind us?"

"It means nothing but Wisconsin." He pointed over the waters off the bow. "My family's over there in the Green Bay area. You think this straights is bad? Now, that's dangerous water over there, for sure. Hundreds of ships have sunk there. They'll need lights to guide them safely in. After this trip's done, I'm going to help build a lighthouse along the Devil's Doorway coast and maybe even be a lighthouse keeper." He grinned. I'd never seen him look so happy. It passed as he leaned close to me and in a low voice said, "I'm more suited for land, if you know what I mean, Honor. Mind you, I love the sea. I love it better with my feet firmly on the terra firma and looking out at it. It's beautiful, but dangerous. You've got to respect her."

Perhaps he thought a city boy like me would prefer land, too. I actually was surprised to find how much I liked the adventure with the uncertain temperament of the sea. People depended on you here – both the passengers and the people who owned the cargo. Even the crew depended on each other to complete jobs.

I decided after I checked up on my sisters to make sure they were in a good family, I'd come back to the lakes and sign on to be a deckhand on some other ship. With my experience and skills gained aboard the *City of Cheektowaga*, surely any first mate would want to hire a strong young lad like me. I turned to start below.

"Welcome to the Stinking Water," William said.

"Stinking Water?" I repeated. Apparently, William was not done.

I sniffed twice over the rail. I didn't notice any stink. I looked at William out of the sides of my eyes. Being so close to Wisconsin made him downright chatty.

"The first European explorers in this area were French, you know," William said.

I rolled my eyes. Of course, I remembered that. "LaSalle," I answered.

"Well, there were others before him," William said. "They had Indian guides, but claimed the land and water for France of everywhere they explored. On the earliest of their French maps, they called this huge body of water 'Lac du Puans,' which means Stinking Lake."

I sniffed again. No odd smell. I squinted at him.

"It's true," he said defensively, holding up his palms. "A little later, the maps labeled it 'Lac du Ilinoi' after the Indian tribe."

I bit the inside of my cheek as I thought. "So what's it called now?" I asked, "'Lac du Cheektowaga?'"

William laughed so hard that I thought he'd fall right over the rail. I folded my arms and stared at him.

"This is Lake Michigan," he said.

Finally, something I knew something about, even if I was from New York. "Named after the state… or maybe the territory," I added quickly. I'd be jiggered if I'd let him have all the right answers. "Maybe one of those snake monsters died nearby and that's what they smelled when they named it."

He shrugged. "I don't really know," he answered.

I grinned. He wasn't all-knowing.

"I do know this," he continued. "The word 'Michigan' is a French form of an Ojibwa Indian word meaning 'large water' or 'large lake.'"

I looked westward and agreed with those smart Indians. This certainly was a large lake.

"So, you're not planning on signing on again when we reach Wisconsin?" I asked.

William shook his head quickly. "I've had enough sea adventure. I'll be heading home."

"Me, too."

He nodded, and then jerked his head to look behind us. I swung around to see First Mate Finbarr standing not three feet behind us. I wondered how long he'd been standing there.

"You jabber like two women. Check and tighten the lines. We're in for a bit of bad weather."

Chapter Sixteen
THE BEAVER ARCHIPELAGO

Finbarr spoke correctly about the bad weather, undoubtedly one of the reasons he was the first mate.

A wall of grey-white clouds advanced towards us from the northwest. The waves swelled to about ten feet tall with thirty feet between. Sailing on calm lakes was fun. Sailing over waves taller than I could see over caused my heart to race.

Captain Klaus remained at the helm during this time, taking the waves at an angle, checking for nearby ships on the crests. Always watching our ship, port to starboard, top of masts to top deck, and keeping an eye on our cargo.

"Thousands of ships disappear in this crack," Finbarr said in my ear. "But not to worry. These lakes can give our captain the worse they can and he always finds his way through. Smooth sailing."

This was smooth sailing?

I rubbed my arms, wanting to rub off my fear. As I lost my balance, I smacked into Mr. Finbarr. He pushed me away.

"Secure the bow lines," he yelled.

Jack and Bernard were doing the same midship. The storm blew stronger. There wasn't going to be warm food from our stove until this storm let up. We held tight, moving with the ship, bracing against each spray.

"It's safer going around the islands," William said, "out to the deep sea."

I wondered if the deep sea had deeper waves.

"Going between the mainland and islands like this cuts off about sixty nautical miles."

Apparently, other ship captains thought the same. From the crests, several ships sailed in this lane.

"That's Beaver Island we're passing by."

"Passing by!" I shouted. Most of the other ships aimed for the island. The grey-white cloud overtook us. We were pelted with snowflakes. "Why don't we make for safe harbor?"

William licked his lips and looked back to our captain at the stern. His shadowy form through the storm resembled a statue.

"Apparently, Captain Klaus doesn't like the king over there."

I tilted my ear closer while hanging onto a rope with one hand and the rail in the other.

I shouted to William over the wind. "I thought you said 'king.'"

William nodded, eyeing the island to our starboard. It seemed like he wished we could be making port there as well.

"Truly, Honor. A king, right here in the United States of America. Lives over there on Beaver Island."

"No."

"Yes. His name is Jesse James."

"That outlaw from the west?" Now I knew he was fibbing.

"No. His full name is Jesse James Strang. He changed his name around to distinguish himself from that western bank robber. He's a Mormon, converted over from the Baptist faith. When the head of the Mormon Church, Joseph Smith, died, Mr.

Strang decided to crown himself King of the Kingdom of God on Earth. It happened just four years ago, right over there. Our own American king."

I wasn't sure what to say to that, so I kept quiet.

"He makes his females followers wear their dresses – or shifts, rather – right up to here." Bernard motioned his hand at his knees. His knees! "With no pantaloons or leggings." I was glad my sisters were far, far away from this obscenity. "I don't think the other Mormons living off island quite agree with him. Captain Klaus would rather put in port anyplace except Saint James Bay."

"You mean, he's a saint as well as a king?"

A cold wave smacked us and knocked me off my feet. I slid back towards midship. The ship listed and the logs slid towards me.

"Honor!"

I scrambled up a rat line as the logs slammed against the starboard side. I hung out over cold Lake Michigan. Captain Klaus spun the wheel like a mad man to straighten us up. I climbed down and clung to the ropes as my feet slid on the slippery logs.

"I'm going below," I yelled to William. He was on watch. I didn't need to be there.

I hung tightly to the ladder and descended to the crew's quarters, praying those big logs wouldn't slide right overtop the hatch and seal me in. Our hammocks swayed, nearly smacking Jack against the wall. He couldn't be sleeping, but he did look peaceful as a sleeping babe. It looked like one of his ropes might give way.

A sailor's knot give way? Whatever was I thinking?

I dried off with my wool blanket. I couldn't tell if I still shook because of the damp cold or from nearly getting crushed.

I left him and dove into the security of my hold. Who should I find there but Old Salty. He danced on one foot and then the other, right down the center of the deck, singing some old sailor tune.

"Honor, me bucko. Glad you came to join the party."

We hit a wave hard and the bow rose. I fell to my face. Old Salty laughed and kept on dancing.

"No, I—" I noticed the ship leaked. How long had it been since I'd checked on it? I grabbed a tin of pitch and pushed it into the cracks between the planks. "You could help, you know," I shouted over my shoulder to Old Salty. He laughed and kept on dancing without missing a step no matter what the ship gave to him. He was just a stowaway, but he still was on board the *City of Cheektowaga*. His life depended on a ship that didn't leak. Didn't he know that?

Water slushed back and forth through the ballast just below the floorboards.

"No need to worry, laddie. The water be a'helpin' to balance out this fine lady. For she be top-heavy-like."

Every bone and muscle in my body was spent. I longed for some soft flour bags to plop onto. I lay on the hold's floor hugging the planks and let the waves and ship rock me. I must have fallen asleep.

"There you are, you good-for-nothing scallywag!" A lantern swung in the hatch opening. Finbarr bellowed at me, "All hands on deck. We're making for a safe harbor."

Chapter Seventeen
SOUTH MANITOU ISLAND

The waves had changed to sharp tops of twenty feet with white caps. Each wave crest sent spray over our ship. The wall of wind struck with bone-chilling depth, bringing snow with it. We were the only ship in sight. Either the others had already made it to a safe harbor, or had fallen down into the crack. Panic rose from my stomach. I wanted to ride out the storm in the hold. I also didn't want to be below deck in case we crested one wave, and then kept going down the other side straight to the bottom of the lake. At least topside I'd have a chance to jump in the yawl. We tossed more lines over the logs attempting to hold them in place. Even with my heavy boots on, the snow mixed with water spray made the deck slippery. I jumped onto he logs once, narrowly missing getting crushed.

Finbarr shouted orders through the wind as Klaus steered. We lowered some of the sails so the wind wouldn't keel us over.

It seemed to take hours to reach the island. We sailed between two of them.

"South Manitou," William shouted.

We hauled down more sail as we shot into the port where many ships had been wiser sooner than we. There were no empty spots left along the docks, and no tugs risking their own lives to come to help guide us in. Captain Klaus sailed into port under half-sail before yelling, "Down all sheets and drop anchor!" shortly before we butted against a steamer.

The screech of wood against wood pierced the air over the wild wind. The bump flattened me against our logs. They cursed at us, but also threw us lines and accepted ours in order to tie together. There didn't appear to be damage to either ship. Captain Klaus jumped aboard their ship as the rest of us secured our sails in the snow storm. The cold turned my hands to ice. I could hardly feel them to form the knots. But somehow we managed, sail by sail.

We were the fifth ship tied sideways, and next to the *Flying Cloud*. I wondered if this was the same ship Old Salty was on when they found the *Jamestown*, but thought that his was a schooner or bark, not a steamer. There must be more than one ship named *Flying Cloud*. It could make for some confusion.

Bernard climbed over each of the ships to go ashore and find some food supplies. Klaus and Finbarr met with other captains and officers on the first ship tied to the dock. Jack went to his hammock while William and I went into the hold to pump out the water we'd taken in. Old Salty was nowhere to be seen.

"I'll be glad when this trip is over," William said, shaking the water and snow from his jacket." "Those waves and snow were starting to worry me some."

"Some? Let's not talk about it." I was starting to sound like an old superstitious sailor.

We worked without talking for a while.

"Something's been troubling me," I said at last.

"Why the captain tricked you into joining us?"

"No. I figured he needed me. He didn't have to be sneaky about it, though. He could have asked."

"Would you have agreed?"

"Not a chance. My sisters need me."

"So what's troubling you?"

"Bernard," I said. "How come Bernard hates me?"

"I don't think he hates you," William answered.

"Ha!"

"He acts tough," he continued, "but you have to realize he lost his entire family – wife and five boys – in a forest fire. Told me when we were downbound to Buffalo."

"He can't blame me for the fire!" I said.

William laughed at my comment. "No, Honor. I think he blames himself, because he wasn't there to save them. He took a liking to Harold for some reason. Maybe Harold reminded him of one of his little boys or what they would be like when they grew up, if they grew up. I don't know. But then Harold left, and here you are."

"Here I am," I repeated.

"We should probably rest when we're done here," William said. "My guess is that as soon as the weather clears, no matter what the hour, we'll be the first ones leaving this port. Must keep to the schedule."

His last words sounded exactly like the captain's voice. We laughed.

When we'd pumped out all the water and caulked where we thought needed caulking, we fell into our hammocks. Jack was no longer in the quarters.

I fell into a sleep and dreamed of Bridget and Sissy dancing and laughing in the hold with Old Salty. They looked like marionettes. Their eyes were shiny black beads and they couldn't hear me shouting to them over Salty's singing and moaning. I needed to get them away, get them safe, but every step I took towards them, I slipped backwards. I awoke with a shout, sitting up and bumping my head against Bernard's back above me. Bernard swung his arm downward to hit me, but he missed. He grumbled, rolled over, and went back to sleep. It took me a long time to do the same.

The storm lasted two long days. No other ships came into port after us.

Captain Klaus and Finbarr were rarely aboard during this time. Jack and Bernard were on again and off again, exploring the town and the other ships and their mates. However, the wind, rain, and sometimes snow flurries kept William and me hunkered down below deck. We played a lot of cards, sang songs, I learned new knots, and we told stories. I even gave William a few chills with my repertoire of ghost stories.

In the middle of the second night, Finbarr woke us with shouts and shakes of our hammocks. I pulled on my sea boots and stumbled topside with the others. Gone were the clouds. Stars studded the black sky. More noticeable was the flickering waves of greens and pinks on the northern horizon. I stared, mystified at what it could be. I'd never seen anything like it in my life. Whatever it was held me spellbound.

"Aurora borealis," William whispered next to me.

I jumped. I'd forgotten he was even there. The sight before me blocked any curiosity of the strange words he spoke.

"They're called the Northern Lights," he explained.

So it wasn't the end of the world. Nor a dream.

"If you don't get moving immediately," shouted Finbarr, "you will get your pay docked."

His words snapped me to another reality. I didn't know until that point that I would actually get paid. Maybe he was just speaking to William. If I got money for this voyage, I wouldn't have to worry about transportation between Milwaukee and Dowagiac.

Jack and Bernard hoisted the anchor with a "heave-ho" song and tossed a line to the waiting tug. The steamer beside us had started up its noisy engine. Smoke poured from its stack. Sailors on all the ships talked and shouted. With William, I scurried onto the logs and up the rope ladder to unfurl the lower sails. I climbed towards a dancing night rainbow. I worked my fingers to undo the knots to the rhythm of those Northern Lights.

As the tug pulled the *City of Cheektowaga* out of the harbor first, followed and quickly passed by the steamer. They didn't blow their horn or jeer at us. I suppose we were anxious to get on with our own journeys. We aboard our ship awaited the order to unfurl the rest of the sails.

William shot me a whispered, "That looks like an eagle."

The sky above me waved. "That looks like a living piano keyboard," I said.

"And that looks like a whip," came Finbarr from below us, "which is what you lot deserve if you don't quit looking up."

Safely out of the harbor, the tug returned for another sailing ships.

The wind filled our sails and we clipped along at a fast pace. We passed the steamer. All our sails and a fine steady wind was no match for any propeller or side-wheeler. We sailed along the Michigan shoreline until we reached Point Betsie. People were building a lighthouse there. Light towers were a wave of the future, and would save many lives. Finbarr kept us well-away from her dangerous point. Captain Klaus turned over the wheel to Finbarr.

"No need to wake anyone," Finbarr told me as my shift ended. "There's nothing now between Milwaukee and us."

Milwaukee. It wouldn't be long until I was off this ship and on my way to find my sisters.

Chapter Eighteen
OPEN WATER

I fell into my hammock ready to fall instantly asleep. Only Jack snored. I sensed the other two were awake, but they were silent.

"I have a bad feeling," Bernard said quietly from his hammock.

I thought he was talking in his sleep, but there wasn't the normal breathing or snoring associated with slumber. William looked over at us. I hoped I didn't look as concerned as he did. Although the ship felt fine, and were we're leaking now, my heart beat picked up at tough old Bernard's words. He was a career sailor. He knew things William and I never could.

I bit my lip and stared at his back above me. After a long time, Bernard continued.

"I don't want to be buried at sea."

"Are you sick or something?" William asked.

"No. I have this feeling."

"Nothing's going to happen," William assured Bernard, or assured himself. "Hundreds of ships sail these seas every day, and the weather looks great."

"And hundreds fail to make port," Bernard answered.

"Harold warned me. He wanted me to get off this ship with him. He knew something would happen. If I die at sea, I won't get my last rites."

The *City of Cheektowaga* creaked. On such a perfect night, it seemed few of us could sleep.

"Nothing's going to happen!" William said louder.

We were no longer in the shipping lane. If something did happen, there'd be no ships around to respond. I swallowed hard and thought how hard it would be on Sissy and Bridget not to know what happened to me. I, too, wouldn't be able to receive my last rites. And then it dawned on me.

"You're Catholic?" I asked. Bernard didn't answer, but I heard him muttering. It sounded very much like the rosary.

I tried to picture Bernard squeezed into a cassock and waving incense over the congregation. I tried to imagine him as a father playing with his children. I couldn't.

"All right," said William through the dark. Jack snorted, and then fell back to his rhythmic snores. "I'll just say this once as long as we're on the subject. If something happens to me on this trip, you two have to see that my body gets back to Green Bay. Promise."

It a silly thing to promise seemed in the case of a disaster, but both Bernard and I grunted a yes, and William sighed heavily as if relieved.

"I want Mary to have one place to go to mourn me and not just to the shore looking out at this big old lake never knowing what happened to my body."

"Maaaary?" I said staring in his direction. "You never told me about Maaaary."

"Just go to sleep."

"Maaaary," I whispered.

Bernard chuckled.

In the dawn, Bernard pulled out foods to prepare breakfast. Jack was at the wheel. The day was too pleasant to be below, and the night's fears had vanished.

Sailing on open water invigorating me. With the winds in your favor and the waves cooperate, and the fall sun beaming down upon you. With no land to show the changing colors of the trees, and no snow blasting at you, it almost felt like a summer day. An Indian Summer day.

After I checked on my sisters, maybe I'd sign back on another ship. I know how to sing and tie knots. I know how to pull down sails, and lift up anchors. I could become a sailor, like Bernard. Sailing through life like, especially on days like this, would be pleasant. Working my shifts would be a breeze, and rocking to sleep, peaceful. I could easily make a career of a sailor. Maybe someday I'd own my own ship.

As Bernard fixed our pancakes, he sang a song about an ash grove of trees. His deep, bass voice vibrated through my being. It was a beautiful song and a beautiful day.

We also were no longer alone on Lake Michigan. Klaus had brought us back into a shipping lane. A bark and another schooner headed west in our direction. A steamer came towards us about a quarter of a mile off. I felt safe to be among other ships again. In a few hours we'd be in Milwaukee and I'd be off this ship with coins in my pocket, on my way to Sissy and Bridget.

"You may have done too good a job of pumping us out back on South Manitou," Finbarr said to me. "With this top heavy load, we need water in the hold to keep better balance. Bernard, go check the water in the hold."

"No."

My eyes widened at Bernard's blatant disobedience to the first mate. Finbarr's mustache twitched.

106

"I haven't finished cleaning breakfast." Bernard held up his bucket of water.

"You are a coward, day or night," Finbarr said.

Bernard's fingers whitened on the bucket handle. I thought he was going to smash it over the first mate's head.

"I'll go," I volunteered, rising and heading for the fore hatch before either Finbarr or Bernard could respond.

I ducked into the hatch, made my way around the plank lumber and down the lower hatch to the near-empty hold.

"Hey, ho, Honor, me lad."

Old Salty did a jig on the deck. He was like a bad penny that kept coming back to me. Was he planning to stowaway aboard the *City of Cheektowaga* forever? I ignored him and knelt on the edge of the deck to check the water level. It was low.

"Did I be tellin' ye about the captain's wife who be gettin' drowned, and now her face be floatin' up the mast in the sheets?"

"I'm just here to check the water," I stated matter-of-factly. "Then I need to report."

Old Salty stood perfectly still. I couldn't hear his boots as he danced any more. Did I ever hear them? What I could feel was his eyes on the back of my head.

"How about the little boy who went down with his ship in a fog and whenever a fog comes over his burial spot-like, people be hearin' his pitiful cries for help?"

"I haven't time for a story," I snapped. I didn't care what the old man thought of my rudeness. All he was interested in was telling his stupid ghost stories. Oooo. I was so scared! I was a sailor now, and I had my duties to do, including a top heavy ship.

Salty spoke low and slowly. "Not even the one about the old sailor, who after decades of trips without incident, be drownin' down in the hold-like?"

"I said, no stories." There was less water down here than Finbarr would want. The ship tilted to the side, then back again. Would we need to bring buckets of water down here to help the ballast.

"Don't ye be likin' spendin' time with me, Honor lad?" Old Salty frowned and his eyes flickered orange.

"No," I snapped. The ship's balance was crucial.

Old Salty's eyes opened wide as he sucked in a breath. I regretted my sharp reply. "I mean, it's been fine. Your stories have been a nice distraction."

"I be merely a distraction for ye? Here. I be a'hinkin' all this time that we be mates and all."

"No, we're not mates. You be a stowaway, Salty, and I be a'gettin' off this ship really soon-like. When we land in Milwaukee, I'll collect my pay and go find my sisters."

He moaned and backed away further into the shadows.

Why didn't he understand? I rolled my head and flung my arms out to my sides. When I looked back to where he'd been, he wasn't there. I looked to my left and right. That old guy moved fast.

"There are more important things in life than telling stories," I said with raised voice. "Like family."

Silence. The dark hold seemed unusually quiet. Even the ship's sides didn't creek.

I scanned along the hull as far as I could make out in the very dim light. Maybe he'd slipped below with the dry ballast.

"My sisters —" I started. My throat choked up. *They're my life*, I thought, as I wiped a renegade tear from my cheek. Now I not only felt bad about my sisters, but also about an old pirate-talking sailor.

TALES OF THE LOST SCHOONER

"Salty?"

No answer.

"Sorry," I muttered.

I climbed up the ladder to report to Finbarr. Bernard was at the helm and William in the bow. White caps moved quickly towards us from the western horizon. I could no longer see the steamer. The wind slammed against me.

Chapter Nineteen
THE GAGGER

"Storm!" I yelled. The wind blew the word from my mouth and the ship lurched to the port. The lumber slid about two feet to the port side. The *City of Cheektowaga* straightened back up. The sky jagged with sideways lightning above us.

"Take the wheel," Bernard said over the wind.

He climbed the stern mast. The waves tried to wrest the wheel from my grip. The wind slammed us from the north. The wheel spun wildly out of my control.

The ship pitched to the starboard. The lumber slid back to where it belonged, leveling our schooner. We'd turned ninety degrees. I was turning us back into the waves when red-faced Klaus bolted through the rear hatch and took the wheel.

"Sails!" he screamed at me.

I scurried up the center mast. If the sails dipped into the water, they could pull us into the sea. William was already up the foremast. Bernard had the sails lowered in the stern and joined me.

Another blast of wind from the west. The squall hit us broadside and we tilted to the starboard. Lightning flashed. The main mast cracked. I covered my head. I was knocked to the deck.

"Run, laddie," I heard Salty say.

I ran along the shifting timber to the bow. We rolled and I fell into the icy water. It was quieter under the surface. Peaceful. I went down and down.

"Kick off yer heavy sea boots, Honor, lad. Kick 'em off!"

I didn't wonder that I heard Old Salty's familiar voice under water. It didn't even sink in that I was in the lake and didn't know how to swim. I was given an order. I obeyed.

"Kick now, Honor, Kick upward."

The water resisted my kicks and moved me upward. I burst through the water's surface, gasping air into my lungs. One of the logs floated in front of me. I scratched at it, but couldn't get a hold. It rolled and tossed on the stormy lake. It slammed into another log right where I'd been holding.

I splashed. I floundered. Water rushed into my mouth.

"Here, Honor," Salty called out again. "Grab hold."

Something bumped my arm. I reached over it. The square lid of the fore hatch. I flung my other arm over and clung to it as I coughed out water.

"Good laddie," Salty whispered. "That's all right now. Kick away from the ship or it'll pull ye down with her suction."

I kicked.

"Now call out for the boat."

It's a ship, I thought. Through the darkness and wild waves, lumber bounced front of me. The *City of Cheektowaga* lay on her side. I heard someone scream as logs slammed into each other. Then there was silence except for the storm.

"Call out!" Salty said more firmly.

"Boat!" I choked out.

"Honor? Honor, speak again." It was William.

Old Salty grinned at me from the other side of the hatch. He wasn't holding onto the wood, but somehow effortlessly stayed afloat. In fact, he didn't look wet.

"Live, Honor Patrick Sullivan," Salty said. "Find those sisters of yours, and live."

A wave splashed over us. I only closed my eyes for a moment. When I opened them, Old Salty was gone.

"Grab the oar," William shouted from the yawl.

I took hold of the outstretched oar and he pulled me to the boat and yanked on the back of my coat to get me in.

"Salty!" I blubbered. "We've got to get Old Salty." I searched the water, but only saw the hatch lid floating away from us. Lumber smashed against each other. All other trace of the *City of Cheektowaga* was gone.

"There!" I called and pointed. "Look! Someone's splashing over there!"

William rowed in the direction.

Bernard latched his hand to my arm and almost pulled me in the drink. He threw a leg over the edge of the yawl and the boat tilted dangerously to the side as water rushed in.

"Stop, Bernard," William said. "Just hang onto the side. A steamer's coming this way. Captain!" he shouted into the storm. "Finbarr! Jack!"

"Salty!" I cried out.

They both looked at me.

"He's a stowaway," I explained. "He stayed down in the steerage hold."

"No one was down there," Bernard screamed at me. "No one!" He shivered. "Only that creepy feeling of someone watching me. What was that?" he yelled. "Someone just grabbed my ankle!"

He thrashed and threw his leg over the side of the boat. William and I leaned hard to port side to keep it from turtling. Bernard clambered aboard the yawl along with half of Lake

Michigan.

"Salty!" I plunged my arm over the side.

"Get your hand out of that water, Honor Sullivan," William commanded. "There's no one alive down there. And end of discussion until we're safely aboard the steamer."

"If ever," Bernard added as I withdrew my arm from the lake. "I don't even care for having only this thin bit of wood between me and ghosts."

Ghosts?

The steamer came in sight. William stood and yelled.

I looked over our ship's debris field and saw him once more. Old Salty flapped his arms as he balanced on top of a rolling log. He stopped suddenly and looked right at me. The log continued to roll beneath him. His eyes glowed as he whispered across the water in a low, creepy voice, "Live."

And then he vanished.

William and Bernard shouted and waved to the steamer. It blasted its horn. With a bit of bashing and smashing, they pulled us three aboard the steamer.

I clung to the rail with a blanket wrapped about me. My rescuers urged me below. I searched the timber for my friend. I wanted to tell Old Salty I was sorry about our last conversation. I never saw him again, but I would find Sissy and Bridget, and live, just as Old Salty ordered me to do.

I turned to William beside me. "So far," I said to him, grinning, "this is the farthest west I've ever been."

THE END

EPILOGUE

The steamer rescued the three survivors in the yawl and took them on to Benton Harbor, Michigan.

Honor did find his sisters in Dowagiac. Sissy had been placed with a family in town, and Bridget with a farm family. Honor never located Chas nor knew what became of him.

Although Honor himself was never placed with a family, he remained in the Dowagiac area for several years doing odd jobs and watching out after his sisters best he could. Bridget married a boy from the farm next door and they had eleven healthy children. Sissy became a hat maker with Hale's Millinery Department in South Haven, and contently lived out her spinster life.

Honor never shared about that someone he conversed with on lonely nights when he was twelve years old aboard the *City of Cheektowaga*. Although he thought about Old Salty now and again, he eventually came to believe Salty was part of his childhood imagination of being separated from his two sisters.

As an adult, Honor took a position as a lightkeeper near Ludington, Michigan. Even as an old man, he remained in contact with another lighthouse keeper on the other side of the lake in Wisconsin, his friend William.

HISTORICAL NOTES

Is it true?

Several people have asked this author, "Are they true?" The difficulty with the question is that I'm not sure if they refer to the shipwrecks, the ghosts, or the story.

My story is fictional, as well as the characters.

However, ships carried passengers, or cargo, and sometimes both, like the *City of Cheektowaga* throughout the Great Lakes since the 1600's. The stories of shipwrecks, when ship names are mentioned, are indeed true historical tragedies. That people hear cries or screams or see something (a person or a ship which disappears) is also true, that is, according to their reports. So, the shipwrecks are true, the story is fictional, but ghosts or ghost ships? That is up to you to decide.

The Orphan Trains

The Children's Aid Society began in New York City by the Reverend Charles Brace, who felt children would fare better if placed with families v.s. in institutions like prisons or mental wards which were the only alternatives at the time. He formed The Children's Aid Society, which was the forerunner of today's Foster Care, and arranged for children to go to homes "on the western frontier." The first group for the Orphan Trains, as they were later called, went from New York City the Hudson River on a side-wheeler steamship called *Isaac Newton* to Albany. From Albany, they went to Buffalo, and then aboard a ship to Detroit, Michigan, where they rode a freight train to their destination in Dowagiac, Michigan. One boy of the forty-seven in the first group was given to the captain of the *Isaac Newton* for use for his sister.

There are very few records of what happened to the approximately 250,000 children, mostly from New York City and Boston, who were "placed out" in many states from the years 1854 to 1926, including in forty-four Michigan cities.

Tales of the Lost Schooner is one author's imagination of what might have happened to one of these lost boys.

Ship Names

Ships in the Great Lakes. were often named after cities, like the *City of Alpena* or the *City of Erie*. The name the *City of Cheektowaga* comes from a town which borders Buffalo, New York. It was settled in the early 1800's, and the town was legally formed in 1832. Whether there was ever a ship named that which sailed on the Great Lakes, this author could not affirm.

Sailor Superstitions

Many sailors are a superstitious lot. Voyages starting on Fridays, salt, coins, names of ships, ghosts – these are all real life in a sailor's lot in the 1800's.

Are superstitions limited to the 1800's? Can you think of superstitions people today may believe?

DISCUSSION QUESTIONS

1. What is Honor's main goal? Does he achieve it?

2. Name three major characters in the story and list their qualities and characteristics.

3. Name the Michigan ports where the *City of Cheektowaga* stopped and what was her cargo. Research other types of cargo on the Great Lakes in the 1800's.

4. If school was not required, but twelve-year-old you needed money to feed yourself or your family, what are some jobs you could do in the 1800's? How about in the 2000's?

5. Who is Old Salty?

TWO LITERARY TREASURE HUNTS

1. Within this book are snatches of old songs from the 1800's. Find the song references and lyrics of traveling on the Erie Canal, or what happens with a drunken sailor, or of a loved one sailing over the sea.

#2. Sometimes, when referring to feeding babies or thirsty adults, we use the expression "down the hatch." Can you picture the parallel between open mouths and the hatch opening of a ship?

Sprinkled throughout the story are old expressions similar to this one, passed down through the generations. How many can you find?

Research to discover the original meanings of these expressions and what they continue to mean even today.

SEA SHANTIES (work songs)

When sailors of the 1800's raised or lowered heavy sails or lifted anchors, the sea shantyman often led them in songs to keep the beat and get them to work (or pull) together. A good seaman was known by his singing voice.

Who was the shantyman in *Tales of the Lost Schooner*?

How many sea shanties are listed in this story? Can you find other verses?

Research to find more lyrics and tunes of this old way of doing team work.

TALKIN' IN PIRATE-SPEAK

Lesson #1 – Talk in present tense. (Not "We were sailing past the island when…," but instead, "We be sailing past the island when….")

Lesson #2 – Drop the "g" from "—ing" words. ("We be sailin' past the island when…")

Lesson #3 – Now and again add "—like" to the end of nouns. ("We be sailin' past the island-like, when…")

Lesson #4 – Sprinkle your speech with piraty phrases. ("Aye, me hearty, we be sailin' past the island when, shiver me timbers, but I spies…")

Lesson #5 – Body language and voice. When you talk, look and sound like a pirate. You could close one eye and squint with the other. Tilt your head a bit to the side, and speak from the back of your throat. OR if ye rather be a gentleman pirtate-like, then be standin' tall and talkin' all pretty-like.

A WORD ABOUT PIRATES
(from the author)

Pirates were thieves, kidnappers and murderers on the water – in other words, dirty, rotten, immoral people. There were also a number of female pirates who were not at all nice. Pirates chased down merchant ships and stole their goods and money. They often killed the people aboard, or "enlisted" them (made them work for the pirates), or threw them into prisons.

When thinking about a typical pirate, a lot of people picture them as coming from the Spanish Main (or Caribbean, off the coasts of Florida and Cuba), dressed in 1700 clothes, and with an exotic pet bird from those parts (like a parrot) sitting on their shoulders. But thieves, kidnappers and murderers have been around long before that era, and the very reason the United States started their navy, to protect merchant ships and US citizens from... say it with me: pirates!

Did you know that even today, there are pirates – and they don't speak in pirate speak, either, but they aren't very nice in the least.

PIRATE GAME
(Similar to Capture the Flag)

Aye, me buckos, pretendin' to be pirates can be all fun-like. Ye can be dividing up into two teams-like with one side pretendin' to be the good guys who have the gold, and the other side pretendin' to be the bad guys who be wantin' the gold. Argh.

The first team must try to get the treasure past the other team and to their own land (line).

The captain of each team be the Sinker. When the captain be taggin' someone from the other team, they must sit (sink to the bottom of the sea) until they be rescued-like by a fellow team member a'touchin' them.

Which side will be sailin' away with the treasure?

ABOUT THE AUTHOR

Sandy grew up boating on the Great Lakes. She loves and appreciates each of the five in their unique ways. She also grew up telling ghost stories to her siblings, cousins and friends, usually seeking out the darkest spaces of houses. She's lived in Cleveland, in Buffalo, and in Michigan, a state with 3,126 miles of freshwater coastline.

Filled with the wonder of history, longing adventure on the inland seas, and the love of story-telling, she'll be a'tellin' stories until the day she dies.

21639015R00068

Made in the USA
Charleston, SC
27 August 2013